JUMP TO THE MOON

By

BORIS PUKIN

Biography

Boris Pukin was born in 1945 in the Urals in the city of Krasnoturyinsk. Boris's grandfather, Colonel Lev Borodyansky, worked as deputy director of a huge plant that produced aluminum. When the whole family moved to Moscow, in 1946, he was arrested on false charges and exiled to the Gulag for 15 years.

Boris went through all the stages of Soviet education: kindergarten, school, technical school and institute. In 1965, he was drafted into the army, where he gave more than three years to the Soviet Union. In 1968, he returned to civilian life and married later that same year.

While working as an engineer, he began writing poetry and prose in 1975. In 1980, a selection of his poems was set to be published in the magazine Youth, but Boris chose freedom instead. In 1981, he emigrated to America with his wife and son, and later that year began working as a designer at a design firm in New York. After retiring in 2017, he continued to engage in creative activities, the fruit of which is the books "A Naughty Life", which was published in 2024, and "Jump to The Moon", which you are now holding in your hands.

To My Grandchildren

Annotation

This book is about children and for children. About actions and misdeeds. About what is good and what is bad. Some of the works included in this book are based on my biography and the biography of my family members, and some are fiction. But the most important thing is that they all carry the same idea — you enter the world of adults and must understand that all your actions and deeds committed in childhood are the foundation on which your entire future life will be built.

Special thanks to my granddaughter Farrah for help with this book.

Table of Contents

Airport

Have you ever seen an airport from a bird's eye view?

Airplanes, like clumsy May beetles, slowly crawl – pausing at times – toward an incomprehensible creature: the passenger station. They press against it and stand still for a while, resting from their labors.

Different-sized machine ants scurry between the beetles, each with its own task. Some take care of the transporters— long grasses—on which suitcase-crumbs crawl. Others have thread-like hoses, supplying juice-fuel to the wings of the airplanes. A few ants busily load food into the hungry bellies of the beetles.

Little poppy seeds—passengers—one by one disappear into the hole between the beetle's head and its wing. As soon as the May beetle is full, fed, and fueled, something magical happens.

From the field come the firefly regulators. They blink their bright lanterns, guiding the heavy beetle forward. Obeying the light, the beetle slowly crawls onto the path.

Step by step, it makes its way across the field, joining a line of small and huge beetles. Then, one by one, they rush into the sky— buzzing and humming with their wing-engines—carrying their precious cargo to another distant glade. another airport.

And so it goes, from early morning until late evening. One beetle land, coming from far away, while another takes off into the blue sky. Over and over again, in a magical dance of wings, lights, and endless sky adventures.

Cowboy Pistol

Sashka Pugovkin from the third building entrance got himself a cowboy pistol. My son told me this news when he ran home from a walk. Lenka looked ordinary - he could have been hung out to dry on a rope along with his jacket, hat and trousers. Mom, as usual, expressed herself quite definitely on this matter– "There is nothing else to walk in, so you will sit at home all day!"

This phrase, which always threw our son into a trance, did not make any impression on him this time. Lenya very quietly and politely replied, "Okay," and went to his room. This was so unexpected for us that we looked at each other in silence, exchanging meaningful glances.

For an hour, mysterious rustling sounds were heard from the nursery. And then Lenka came out into the kitchen. His eyes were shining with joy, and over his short pants he was wearing a soldier's belt, which he had traded with someone for some American chewing gum. Two plastic bags were attached to the belt, in which lay various pistols, and on the belt itself were various incomprehensible figures made of plasticine and shiny candy wrappers.

On his feet were rubber boots, and on his head was a homemade **budyonovka.** *(Russian word for the famous cap for Russian army during world war).* Lenya looked at us with a proud look and again went into his room. After a while, gunfire and shouts of "Hurray!" could be heard from inside, from which my wife and I concluded that another general battle was taking place in the room. Hearing the thunder of the battle, my wife told me that although it was not pedagogical to go back on her word, she was willing to let our son go outside for a walk – because we did not have money for new clothes.

When Lenya learned of our decision, he could no longer contain his joy and quickly got dressed and flew out into the yard. We smiled sweetly and went about our business. Less than half an hour had passed when Lenya returned home. He walked into his room with his head down, carrying a homemade cowboy belt in his hands.

At lunch, I asked my son what had happened and why he was so sad. He told me that the boys had looked at his belt and decided that it didn't look like a real one at all, and had chosen Sasha Pugovkin as their commander. Lenya spent the rest of the day sitting quietly at his desk, doing nothing, sadly looking out the window. Late in the evening, when our son was already asleep, my wife and I decided that Lenya needed to buy the same belt with pistols as Sasha Pugovkin had. In the morning, having learned of this wonderful news, he immediately rushed out into the street with the clear intention of telling the boys that he would soon have a cowboy belt with pistols.

On Monday, after taking my son to kindergarten, I went to the local market, Detsky Mir, intending to buy Lenya the promised toy before work. Imagine my disappointment when I found out that cowboy pistols were rarely available. The saleswoman, a nice girl with ink-colored hair, confidentially told me to come back at the end of the month, that is, in about three weeks.

For days, I ran to different shops in vain, trying to buy the ill-fated belt. But as luck would have it, this toy was nowhere to be found. Every evening Lenya met me with the question: "Dad, did you buy me a cowboy belt?" And I, looking away, would tell him that I would definitely buy it tomorrow. But then the end of the month came, and I went to Detsky Mir. Seeing me, the girl with ink-colored hair, with a conspiratorial look, told me that the pistols would be available after lunch. I suffered through half the day at work, waiting.

My stomach was sick, like it used to be before an exam at the institute. At lunchtime I rushed to the store. There was a crowd of people at the counter, and a cowboy belt with pistols was on display in the window. In the evening, I was returning home, carrying a precious toy in my briefcase, and I imagined how happy Lenya would be, and my heart was filled with pride in myself.

I didn't open the apartment door with my key; instead, I pressed the doorbell. Lenya opened it. I entered the hallway, winked mysteriously at my son, and reached into my briefcase. I had just managed to get out the bag with the cowboy pistols, when my son, looking at it, said: "Dad, Sashka Pugovkin's parents bought him an electric submarine."

The Brave Kitten

(fairy tale)

He was the last of his eight brothers and sisters. His mother, whom everyone around called Manka, was a beautiful black cat with a fluffy tail. All the kittens were born as black as their mother, and only our hero was different from his relatives - he was gray with a white tie and white marks on three paws.

The kitten did not have a front right leg. Our little one did not feel any difference yet, because all eight were blind and could not walk. They lay leaning against their mother for most of the day, and when they wanted to eat, they sucked on their mother's warm and delicious milk and quietly purred with pleasure.

From time to time, their dad, a huge black-brown cat named Semyon, would come and bring his catch of voles in his teeth so that Manya could eat. While the kittens were small, the whole family lived in a warm corner behind the stove, where it always smelled of something tasty. However, our hero did not yet know what exactly.

Day after day passed. The kids began to see clearly and learned to walk a little. Oh, it was a fun time of carefree childhood, when you have nothing to do except start the next prank right now. Well, and when the pranks turned into fights, Mom immediately intervened, grabbing the bully by the scruff of the neck with her teeth and carrying him to the corner, where she lay down next to the naughty boy and didn't let him play with his brothers and sisters until the troublemaker calmed down.

By that time, all the kittens had their own names, and of course, our hero, who was named Gray, had one. The baby did not yet understand the full weight of existence that awaits a cat without a paw, but his mother knew how hard life would be for him and pitied him more than anyone else. She affectionately purred his name Gray, and he comically hobbled to her so that she could wash him with her warm, rough tongue and then feed him with her sweet milk.

Semyon the cat spent a lot of time with the kittens, teaching them to jump and run, and they spent hours chasing his tail, trying to catch imaginary prey. Gray's father didn't pay attention. Why? He was not long for this world anyway. You can't run much on three legs. When the kids were learning to catch a tail, our kitten lay in the corner, carefully watching and remembering every movement.

When Father went hunting and the tired brothers fell asleep, Manka called Gray and let him play with her tail, which made the kitten incredibly happy. He tried to jump and run after the elusive fluffy tip, but then the noise woke up his relatives and he would shyly hide in a corner near his mother and quietly – so that no one would see his tears – cry. Time passed, and the kittens grew up a little. Our hero grew up too.

He fell further and further behind his brothers and sisters in his studies and therefore became more and more silent and sullen. The kittens did not want to play with him - they were not interested because Gray always lost in competitions. He lay awake all night long and thought, thought, thought.

That memorable night was no different from any other, but something inexplicable made him get up and go out into the yard. Above his head was a velvety sky, strewn with colored pebble-stars, and above the horizon hung a large yellow-gray bowl, which people called the Moon. He looked around. Everything around breathed silence and peace. The whole world had no time for him.

Gray crawled under the fence and hobbled wherever his eyes looked. He himself did not notice how he found himself on the edge of the forest. He was surrounded by darkness. Unfamiliar smells and voices of birds at first frightened him, but our little hero was not a coward and comically trotted into the forest. He walked for a long time and, tired, stopped in a clearing near a stream.

He drank some cold water and lay down to rest. He was hungry. He sniffed and licked the leaves hanging from a tree branch, but they tasted very bitter. He lay there for about half an hour and just got up to go on, when he stopped, admiring the graceful animals that came out of the forest into the clearing. He did not know that they were deer, but he remembered their smell. He was struck by their presence. They moved across the clearing with small steps, and then suddenly made a jump, which looked more like the flight of a bird without wings, and again continued to slowly walk across the clearing and nibble the grass.

At every rustle, they raised their heads and gracefully turned them, peering attentively into the darkness. The leader of the herd, a large deer with beautiful branched antlers, gave a signal, and the whole group moved further into the forest in the direction of another clearing, which was visible between the trees. The herd moved slowly and Gray, trying to keep up, hobbled behind. When the clearing to which the leader was leading the deer came very close, the animals started to gallop, flying over low bushes to quickly reach their goal: a large clearing, completely covered with a tasty green carpet.

Our kitten fell behind the herd more and more, getting stuck in the grass and clinging to thorny bushes. And suddenly, some invisible force made him jump forward, imitating these beautiful animals, and he, squatting and pushing off the ground with all three paws, flew forward. It was so great that he jumped tirelessly all the way to the clearing. Under a huge old oak tree on the edge of the forest, Gray saw a small field mouse.

Our hungry hero gathered himself into a ball and, with all his might, jumped on the prey. Now he was full. His eyes closed by themselves, and he fell into a sweet sleep. When he woke up, the sun was already quite high and he stretched out on the soft grass and began to think about what to do next. He thought and thought yes. He got hungry again and decided to hunt. Luck came only in the evening. Having had his fill, he galloped to the already familiar clearing, and when he got to the place it was starting to get dark.

Gray lay down on the grass under the hazel bush where he had spent the previous night. Soon, a handsome deer appeared in the clearing, followed by the whole herd emerging from the forest. It was warm and quiet. Nothing foreshadowed trouble, when suddenly the leader raised his head, tensed up, and looked intently toward the old oak.

The kitten stuck his head out from behind the bush and saw two yellow dots on the side where the deer was looking attentively. Gray unmistakably recognized it - it was a wolf! He remembered the smell from the skin lying behind the stove in the house where he was born. Mom often told the kittens to stay away from wolves.

The yellow dots grew closer as a seasoned wolf slowly walked into the clearing. The herd of deer instantly disappeared into the forest, leaving only a proud deer standing before the wolf. Menacingly lowering his head, struck his hoof. Our fearless hero jumped out from under the bush and stood next to the deer. The wolf paid no attention to the baby, who was almost invisible in the tall grass.

The fight did not last long, and the disgraced wolf ran into the forest away from this strong deer with very sharp antlers and powerfully beating hooves. The kitten turned his muzzle toward the leader and, to his horror, saw that he was lying on the grass, blood flowing from a wound on his front right paw.

Without thinking twice, Gray crawled up to the deer and began to lick the wound with his little tongue. Only by dawn did the blood stop oozing and the wound began to heal. The deer found the strength to get up, gratefully licked the kitten's head and limped off into the forest to his deer family. Our hero took a long look in the direction the wolf had run, shook out his matted fur coat, and galloped toward home.

Only by the end of the next day did he see the familiar fence, and, climbing over the lower pole, he limped towards the house. Everything in the hut was just as before - his mother resting on a soft mat, and the stove smelled of something delicious.

Gray drank some milk, lay down next to his mother and thought about how no one had paid any attention to his disappearance. With this sad thought, he fell asleep, and Manka quietly crawled up to her son to warm him with her body. Contentedly tapping her tail on the mat, she dozed off.

Several weeks passed. Our hero grew up and, having learned from the deer, began jumping with all his might, competing in agility and playing with his sisters and brothers. He was happy: the family accepted him into their bosom.

One day, just as the sun was setting, a commotion broke out in the yard. The yard dog, Stepan, was growling angrily and barking mercilessly at someone. All the kittens instantly woke from their sleep and ran outside, where they saw the following scene: Stepan, a big shaggy dog, was guarding his bowl of water, not letting the ducklings near it – and he looked ready to tear their mother, a duck named Sonya, to shreds.

The duck ran from the dog, protecting her children, not knowing how to hide from the toothy mouth. Gray, without thinking, jumped between the duck and the dog, arched his back and, with all his might. meowed. And then something happened that is still gossiped about in the village. Evil Stepan tucked his tail between his legs and, backing away, hid in the kennel so that even his nose was not visible.

The ducklings drank water from the dog's bowl with pleasure and trotted after Mama Sonya to the other end of the yard. Gray straightened up proudly and, raising his head, limped into the house to quickly tell his mother about his heroic deed.

When the kitten entered the hut, the handsome deer standing at the gate raised his head with huge, branched antlers, turned around and ran into the forest to rejoin his herd. Two weeks later, the neighbors came to take the kittens. The owner of the house, a huge man named Timofey, picked up Gray and said to the neighbors: "Here are seven young creatures. Take whoever you want - but this hero will stay with us to guard the hut!"

A Good Fairy Tale

He was born from a very swollen bud. It happened early in the spring, in the morning, when the sun was rising over the roofs of houses, illuminating all living things with its warm rays. The maple tree on which the little green leaf appeared, along with hundreds of its brothers and sisters, grew on the sidewalk of the main street of the city.

This small town was lost among a huge number of similar settlements scattered throughout the territory of this huge and very beautiful country, washed by great oceans from the east and west.

Bathing in the warm rays of the sun, the little leaf quietly rustled - as if singing in its rustling language together with its neighbors, obeying the wind-conductor. And when the wind died down, a small fly would fly in and tease the leaf, landing on it and flying away.

She would tickle it with her claws, and it would pretend to be angry, although it really enjoyed playing with this little bug that didn't know a minute of peace.

The sun would rise higher and higher and become warmer and warmer. Then our little one would doze off, absorbing the life-giving rays of the sun, and would slowly grow up without even noticing it.

The leaf's favorite pastime was watching people. In the mornings, people would hurry to work. Everyone had serious faces - some carried a briefcase, others coffee, and some bags with breakfast. But, in the evenings, they hurried home, to the theater, or to the cinema, and their faces were cheerful, full of anticipation for a pleasant night. When it grew dark outside and the streetlights came on, couples would sit on the benches.

They were whispering about something, hugging and… kissing. In such moments, our hero would become embarrassed and turn away, but nevertheless, his soul became warm and an incomprehensible feeling of joy for these lovers overwhelmed him. All his brothers and sisters did the same as he did, they turned away so as not to disturb the solitude of happy hearts.

One late evening, when the boulevard was empty, two boys approached the tree. One of them pulled a knife from his pocket and began to carve something on the bark. All the branches swayed, as if from a strong wind, though the air outside was completely still.

The poor maple felt a strong pain - this pain penetrated every twig and leaf. Having completed their nasty deed, the boys ran away, and the tree began to cry. Sap flowed from the wound, down the trunk, like the tears of a small, defenseless child. By morning, the pain had subsided, and the wound had healed with amber-colored resin. The leaf promised itself never to hurt the weak or defenseless.

At night, the leaf would curl up into a tube and fall asleep until dawn. As soon as the sky in the east began to brighten, a flock of birds would fly to the tree and sit on the branches like notes on a sheet of music, and begin to sing in all sorts of ways. Our hero loved the bird concert – it set a joyful tone for the whole day.

After all, a whole day is a lot of time for a small green leaf, and for children too. Life seemed wonderful to him, filled with so many fun things that some of them had to be saved for tomorrow, because evening would come, and he would go to bed completely tired, curling up the edges like children tuck their palms under their cheeks, settling in more comfortably before going to sleep.

There was an ant trail running along the branch where our little leaf lived, between the trees, about ten meters from our maple. Small black ants carried bud skins, pieces of fallen leaves and dried bark to their home.

The little leaf did not know why the trail ran along the tree trunk and not directly from the tree roots to the anthill, but he was glad of this circumstance. Watching the ants, as if enchanted, he was amazed at their strength and mutual assistance. They never quarreled with each other and ran to help a comrade as soon as they saw that one of them was in trouble.

The little leaf especially liked one family of ants: a father and three sons. They always worked together, carrying a particularly heavy load, and the leaf, when they ran past it, began to swing like a fan to send a little wind in their direction and cool their bodies, heated by hard work. The ants always thanked it for this, saluting it with their front right paw.

One morning the leaf woke up from a loud noise: a thunderstorm was raging over the town. The peals of thunder, the whistle of the wind, the noise of the rain merged into one monotonous hum. Streams of water rushed along the street where our maple grew and along the sidewalk.

A banana peel, caught on the bark of the tree, told the old branch that it had seen such a downpour only once before, in its homeland, where its banana family lived on a palm tree not far from the equator. An hour later the thunderstorm calmed down and the sun peeked out from behind the clouds, caressing everyone and everything around with its warmth.

It seemed to say: "Calm down, don't worry, I'm with you, everything will be fine." And nature, listening to the sun, calmed down. The leaflet, shaking off the water, watched with interest as the kids, ankle-deep in water, ran along the sidewalk, shouting and laughing. For them, this was an unexpected adventure, and even the stern voices of their mothers could not tear them away from this fun.

The green leaflet laughed merrily, looking at the flushed children's faces, and all the leaves living next to it on the branch laughed with it. Suddenly, through the noise of children's voices, our hero heard a faint squeak. He looked down and right under his branch he saw a familiar family of ants, three sons and a dad, floundering in the water.

They clung to the curbstone, trying to get out of the water onto the tree, but the kids were running out of strength, and their father couldn't help them because he was completely exhausted himself. What happened next, all the leaves on the tree, discussed until late autumn. Our green leaf tore itself off the branch with a sharp movement and glided into the water stream.

Clinging to the sidewalk with its foot, it swam up to the ants and offered them its edge. The whole family, with the last of its strength, climbed onto the leaf. The ants shook off the water, caught their breath and climbed out onto the saving sidewalk, from which the water had already receded. The ant trail began to work again, and they, joining the stream of cheerful workers, dragged blades of grass to repair the anthill.

Our hero, seeing all this, was very happy —but he no longer had the strength to hold on to the maple bark. Breaking away from the tree, he floated along the sidewalk, drifting further and further from the maple where he was born. Rushing to help the ants, he knew what he was doing —there was no turning back! Yet he decided to take this step because he could ignore his comrades in trouble.

The flow of water carried him faster and faster. Our hero floated along unfamiliar streets, past different trees, new faces flashed before him. Tired from the events of the day, he fell into a restless sleep, completely surrendering to the power of the flow. Waking up with the first rays of the sun, the leaflet looked around and was surprised to discover that around him was not the familiar town, but the green banks of a small river.

Other birds flew in the sky, singing songs that were unfamiliar to the ear. There were no people on the riverbanks, although here and there he saw large horned animals peacefully chewing grass. He also noticed that he was beginning to turn yellow, losing his beautiful green color. A few more days passed, and he was already gliding along the wide expanse of water, barely seeing the banks. The leaf turned completely yellow, its edges curled up into a tube, yet it kept floating, and floating, and floating into the beautiful unknown.

.The following spring, little green leaves began to appear from the swollen buds on the old maple. Little green babies also appeared on the branch where the ant trail ran. One day, four little black ants, a father and three sons, crawled onto our branch and, running up to one of the leaves, began to tickle it with their antennae.

The baby liked it very much and gave them water from a drop of dew that was sitting on it. From then on, every day exactly at noon, he greeted his little friends with a drop of dew - pure, as only a child's tear can be. Summer was coming.

Jump To The Moon

"Oh, how cold!", he babbled, inhaling the smell of the grass on which he lay.

Something warm and rough licked his little body. He opened his eyes - his mother was standing next to him.

How do I know this word, Mom? - he thought, but, finding no answer, he began to look around.

Tall sticks poked out of the soft carpet where he was lying, and on them hung many "rustlers" that made a pleasant, soothing sound. A large animal, called "Mom", stuck its warm nose under my tummy and pushed me up. I tried to get up, but my absurdly long legs were in the way. Nevertheless, groaning, I straightened first my back legs, then my front legs, and, comically spreading them out, rose from the grass. Something rocked me to the side, but Mom held my side with her warm nose, and I stayed on my feet.

- "It's the wind," - said Mom, licking my eyes.

I don't know what my eyes have to do with my tummy, but I felt hungry.

- Hurray! I already know the meaning of three words: "Mom, wind and hunger."

Mom was nearby, the wind had stopped blowing, and hunger prevented me from thinking.

- Aha, I need to do something about this very hunger - I muttered, and felt a button on Mom's belly, from which, at my touch, a tasty liquid poured into my mouth. Mom called this deliciousness milk. I continued to suck the button from which this very milk flowed, and somehow, it got into my tummy. - Ha! How interesting, I thought, and stopped sucking the button - I didn't want to anymore.

- Well, well. - I said to myself - Someone is controlling me. But who?

I looked around, there were many beautiful animals in the clearing, like my mother. They were slowly moving and nibbling the soft carpet. My mother caught my gaze and said:

- The soft carpet is called grass. - It is very juicy and tasty. When you grow up and become an adult deer, you will eat it.

- So that means I am a deer? - I asked.

- No. - Mom answered. - You're still a fawn - my son.

Some animals had such beautiful sticks on their heads, especially one huge deer: he had a whole fence on his head.

- And how come these things don't bother him? - I thought.

Turning my head, I looked at myself and discovered that my skin was the same color as other animals, only I was covered in light spots. The big deer explained:

- It's for camouflage. When you sleep during the day, these spots will look like sunbeams and no one will notice you.

- I was just born and already have no peace - everyone is teaching me something. - I muttered, continuing to examine myself.

Rubbing my forehead against a tree, I discovered that I didn't have sticks on my head—excuse me, antlers —yet. All the deer walking around the clearing had this light (what should I call it?) fluff on the other end of their heads. The deer waved it around in a funny, chasing off the buzzing little ones. I felt that I had something back there, behind me, but I couldn't see what exactly.

- How can I look at this "something" behind? Aha! –

- I spread my front legs, bowed my head and stuck it under my tummy. The adult deer in the clearing laughed, and I wanted to be offended, but why, because I had achieved my goal: I had the same white fluff behind me. Mom licked my forehead and said:

- This fluff is called a tail.

I was eight hours old. A warm red circle was rising into the sky and it was getting lighter and lighter around. I lay down on the grass under a bush and at the other end of the clearing I saw a small deer, like me, with light spots.

- I need to go and meet her, I thought, but my eyes closed on their own and I fell asleep.

I woke up when the red circle jumped to the other side of the sky above the clearing. Standing up, I stretched and pressed myself to the button on my mother's belly. The warm, sweet milk quickly filled me up. I felt a surge of strength and wanted to jump, which I did, but, unable to stay on my feet, I clumsily plopped down on the grass.

- Don't rush. - Mom said and showed me how to jump.

I repeated my mother's movements once, twice, three times. and found myself at the opposite end of the clearing, where another spotted fawn was sucking a button from its mother. I stood and watched. It was exactly the same fawn as me, but something was wrong, as if something was missing.

- Ha! - I exclaimed. - It smells different.

Then my mother explained to me that this fawn was a girl.

- And who am I? - My question followed.

- You are a boy. - Mom answered and lowered her head, nibbling on the grass.

- So, we need to come closer and figure out what the difference is between us. - I decided.

Before I could get closer, the girl tore herself away from the button and introduced herself:

- My name is Abi, and yours?

- Charlie. - I muttered in response, examining her carefully.

Abi looked exactly like me, but she smelled different and there was something missing. But what? Not finding an answer, I suggested:

- Let's jump.

She looked at my mother and only after she saw an approving nod, she came up to me.

The forest clearing where the deer were grazing was fenced off from the forest on both sides by two huge boulders. On the other two sides, at the edge of the clearing, stood large deer with branched sticks on their heads. They moved their ears, listening attentively to what was happening behind the trees, while nibbling the grass.

Abi and I were jumping in the middle of the clearing, and the whole herd surrounded us, ready at any moment to protect the children from any danger. The sun hid behind the treetops and the clearing quickly became dark.

- This is very strange, I thought. - It's dark all around, but I can see everything well. I need to figure this out.

But the tummy gave the command again and Charlie jumped up and said:

- Bye. - He ran up to his mother and grabbed the tasty button with his warm soft lips.

Having eaten his fill and falling asleep, he only had time to think:

- I'm already one day old.

I'm one month old. Hooray! I'm already big. Well, at least bigger than I was. A week ago, my friend Abi suggested trying some grass. I really liked the smell of young shoots, and I pinched off a little and ate it. It was very tasty, but you have to chew the grass and it's tiring, and the milk just flows from the button into your mouth, and from your mouth into your tummy - it's so easy and simple.

Drink and you're full! I shared these thoughts with Abi, and she said that I was still small, I didn't understand anything and in general, as my mother says, all males are lazy. Big deal, small! Yes, it is true she's older than me by five whole days, but it is not tactful to remind me of this every day.

Perhaps I will be offended. Pretending that I was very hurt by her remark, I walked away to the side of the bush, where my mother was standing next to our leader. Oh, by the way, our leader's name is Lord Chubs, he is my dad, and the sticks on his head are horns. And I will have such powerful and beautiful horns when I grow up, but many weeks will have to pass before that.

When it got dark, my mother took me to a clearing where I had never been before and explained in detail everything about milk, grass and teeth. Well, now hold on, arrogant girl! Now I know so much that you can't even dream of. In the morning, having drunk milk, I fell asleep, lying on the soft grass under a beautiful bush. I woke up when the sun was in the western part of the sky. The sun is a big bright circle in the sky.

That's what I called it when I was very little, you see. Soon the moon will appear in the sky - that's another circle, only not as bright. When the sun climbs into the sky - that's called day, and I immediately want to sleep. It warms my back and immediately becomes warm and cozy. And, the time when another circle appears in the sky, or half a circle, or nothing at all, is called night. Night is the time for eating, walking in the forest and clearings, and, most importantly, it is the time for games.

Dad told me that at night, two-legged creatures called humans sleep, and during the day they walk and drive very noisy boxes called cars (this word is very difficult to pronounce) and prevent us from resting. And dad also said that humans, instead of horns, wear caps of different shapes on their heads and change them much more often than we change horns.

They have the same substance in their heads as we do, but the problem is that they don't know how to use it. Of course, I'm already big, but I can't understand this philosophy of Daddy, as mom says. There are a lot of spots on the moon tonight, someone has really dirtied it. I tried to jump up and lick these spots off it, but it's very high up, and I don't have enough strength to jump to it yet.

I woke up. The sun, clinging to the tops of the trees, pulls them westward, but they stubbornly refuse to bend, rustling their leaves as they talk to each other. So, it's time to get up. Almost the entire herd is already on their feet. It's time to refuel – my tummy is singing me a feeding song. But what is this?

The leader ordered everyone to gather at a large boulder in the south of the clearing. You can't disobey. The leader's order is the law! I go to the southern end of the clearing, approach my mother and, raising my head, look at my father. He climbed a hillock near a large stone and, proudly raising his head and looking around the herd, said:

- Deer, it's time to leave our home – this cozy clearing, and look for another place to live. Two-legged creatures came to our forest and began to build burrows. Yesterday evening I ordered four deer to go around the forest and find a new camp. When they return, we will discuss the situation and choose a place for a new camp. That's all for now.

Lord Chubs came down from the hill, approached me and my mother, and, hanging his head, said quietly:

- I never thought that I would live to see this day. - And, moving away to the boulder, he thought deeply.

- Abi! - I called and when she came up, I said:

- Let's go look at these new holes and drive the people out of our forest. This is our home! Ah, it's a pity that I don't have horns yet.

She thought and said as calmly as possible:

- Let's go. But first we'll just have a look and that's all.

- Okay. - I agreed.

It was already getting light when we approached the construction site. The construction site is the place where the people will live in their holes. Many bipeds were swarming around in the huge clearing. They sawed, knocked, and shouted. Some of them blew smoke from their mouths and noses, which smelled foul. One of the men climbed into a one-armed monster, at the end of which were huge teeth, and began to dig at the ground.

Having dug up a lot of turf and sand, he moved into another monster and, lowering his single jaw, began to fill in the hole in which the other men had placed iron rods. Strange creatures, these two-legged ones: first they dig a hole, and then fill in the same place. We watched these weirdos for a while, then headed home in the evening. I got a good scolding from my mother after that.

Very tired, I fell asleep without even nibbling the grass. The deer scouts returned and brought bad news. There was only one place where the herd could move, but it was very far away and not in such a nutritious place as our clearing. The leader had something to think about. He gathered all the deer and said:

- We'll leave in four weeks, when the little ones grow up and get stronger. Get ready. - He turned and went into the forest.

White fluff fell from the sky, turning into water, tickling my nose in a funny way. Mom said this fluff is called snow, and that cold weather would soon come. When I woke up, the snow covered the entire clearing – and me too.

I got up, shook myself off and noticed with surprise that the fluff, which is called snow, washed away all the light spots on me. I also saw how Mom pushed this very snow away with her hoof and ate grass. I began to do the same and, without noticing it, ran into the trunk of a pine tree at the edge of the forest.

- What is this? - I thought - Some kind of buns appeared on my head.

Mom, who was standing nearby, explained:

- Charlie, your horns are sprouting.

- Hooray! I'm already a few months old, and I'm almost an adult! – I shouted.

- Don't rush. – Mom said. – You still have time to grow up.

The beginning of March. The sun has climbed to the middle of the sky. I am already as tall as Mom. She is lying next to me, and quietly crying. Dad, having hobbled with difficulty to the trees, stands leaning his side against an old pine tree. As people say, we have big troubles in our family.

Two days before the herd was supposed to be pumped to a new clearing, Dad was hit by a car and his front leg was broken. On that ill-fated night, all the deer in the herd ran out onto the road and helped the leader return to our clearing. I remember the man, who smelled foul, climbed out and swore loudly, examining his car.

That same night, Dad ordered a new leader to be chosen. It was a young strong deer with beautiful antlers, and two days later the herd left for a new habitat, and we were left alone - Dad, Mom and me. After two weeks, Dad's leg wound had healed, but he could no longer run, much less jump. One night, when Mom was grazing on the opposite side of the clearing, Dad said to me:

- Charlie, it won't be long before I go to heaven to be with my parents. I ask you this: take care of Mom until we meet over the rainbow.

He fell silent, lay down on the grass, leaning against a boulder and thought deeply. That night, I promised myself never to leave Mom.

I am one year old. Dad went over the rainbow, and Mom and I were left alone. At a distance of two hours' walk from our clearing, people built many holes and roads. Sometimes I leave Mom alone and go towards the holes, which the two-legged ones call homes. In our deer understanding, home is where it smells of mom, dad and fawns.

For humans, home is a large box made of dead trees, with an artificial sun inside, where noisy little people and animals that look like wolves run around. Yes, the fact that I leave Mom alone is not dangerous for her. Of course, I already have horns and I can protect her… but there is no one to protect her from.

When the two-legged ones came to these places, a pack of wolves and several bears left these places.

Even such strong animals could not live next to people - the two-legged ones have such long sticks from which fire flies and very hard nuts. These nuts hurt us animals a lot, and sometimes even send us over the rainbow. People haven't come to our little piece of forest yet, so I'm not worried about Mom. I shed my antlers for the first time – that means I'm already an adult white-tailed deer.

Of course, I looked better with the antlers, but first, they get in the way of moving through the dense forest and bushes, and second, I have no one to show off to. Mom has grown very old. She looks at the sky more and more often – waiting for her rainbow, dreaming of meeting Dad. I don't want her to leave, because then I'll be all alone. Once, she told me that I look a lot like my father – that I'm as big and strong as he was.

That night I tried to jump high, high again to clear the spots from the moon, but I didn't have the strength for it again. I looked at the bushes I had flown over and realized that I was close to my goal. The time will come, and I will clear this beautiful circle in the sky from dark spots. I am two years old.

Evening. I am standing on a hill by the fence, watching a biped cook food over a fire in an iron thing. The others , big and small people, are sitting at the table, and I can hear them swallowing their drool as they wait to be fed. Strange creatures, these bipeds.

We deer, well… we sniff the grass, find the tastiest patch, and eat it. Simple and tasty. But these creatures need a very long time to study just to understand how to do that. Unfortunately, they have nowhere to learn it. In their educational institutions, children are taught all sorts of things —except not how to find and eat food.

I am standing by the fence, when suddenly an animal runs up to the other side of the fence, barking, almost the size of me and very similar to a wolf, but with a different smell. The four-legged creature stops in front of me and falls silent.

- Samson! – The food gatherer shouts – Come back!

It's not a wolf that takes off running toward the man, then sits down beside him. I think this two-legged creature is the leader of the pack. He strokes the four-legged creature on the head and says something to him. The not-wolf replies:

- Woof! – And runs into the dark corner to the fence where I am standing.

- Hello. I am a dog named Samson. – He introduces himself.

- Good evening. – I answer politely. – My name is Charlie. I am a deer.

- Yes, I know. Yesterday evening, one came by here, such a beautiful one, smaller than you, named Abi. We met. We chatted. She said that she used to live in these parts and that she would visit me in a few days. Don't be afraid of me, I am only scary in appearance, but in my soul, I am kind. It's not for nothing that the breed is called "Kindman".

I love children and I love to chat with different animals. What I don't like are squirrels, they stick their noses into everything. Well, okay, it's time for me to eat. Come again, let's talk about hares. They dig holes on my territory without permission. Bye! Samson ran away, and I thought that we would hardly have met if there hadn't been such a high fence between us.

Charlie returned home in the early morning. His mother was standing in the middle of the clearing, looking at the stars fading in the sky. Her son came up to her, rubbed his cheek against his mother's warm side and asked:

- Can you explain why I'm so sad?

She licked his forehead and said quietly:

- It's time for you to start your own family.

Charlie raised his head and said proudly:

- I'll never leave you! I promised my father this when he went off to find his rainbow.

The sun illuminated the western side of the clearing, and the deer lay down to sleep by a large boulder, next to a hillock where Lord Chubs, the leader of their once large and friendly family, often stood.

A week has passed. At sunset, Charlie ran to the two-legged den again. An incomprehensible feeling made him do it today. He ran at full speed, as if afraid of missing something. He flew up to the fence and stopped dead in his tracks.

- Did you miss me? Ha! - Samson was already waiting for him at the fence and, seeing him, wagged his short tail with joy.

- How are you? - Charlie asked, catching his breath.

- Not great. - The dog muttered. - My whole family has their noses in a box and is watching people shoot each other. But it's all a hoax - I know it.

- How do you know it's a hoax? - The deer asked.

- I can tell by the smell. This box smells of electricity, not blood.

- What is electricity? - Charlie asked.

- I don't know for sure, but I once licked a box with holes in the wall, and it bit me pretty bad. We have a lot of these boxes around our house, and I try to stay away from them.

Suddenly, a shadow separated from the trees and slowly approached Charlie. It was Abi. He recognized her immediately. A slender, beautiful doe who brought with her the scent of childhood.

They stood there, unable to tear their eyes away from each other. Samson realized that he was the third wheel here. Quietly retreating to the dwelling of the two-legged, he lay down by the warm wall and pretended to doze off, resting his head on his front paws and, occasionally opening his eyes, checking if everything was in order in his house.

In the morning, Abi returned with Charlie to the old clearing. In April of the following year, they had a son - Joshua. One warm August night, when there was a full moon, Charlie saw his son jumping comically through the bushes. He came closer and asked:

- Son, what are you doing?

To which the fawn replied:

- Do you see the moon, dad? It is so beautiful, but the dark spots on it spoil everything, and I want to lick them off. But the moon is so high that I can't reach it.

- Be patient. The time will come, and you will definitely jump to it. - Charlie said, looking at his mother and Abi, and tears welled up in his eyes.

Hedgehogies are People Too

In a dense grove, under a spreading bush, lived an old hedgehog named Khryukhryu, translated into human language as Goodman. He was many years old and a little older. He lived all alone in his cozy hole. His girlfriend, Khrokhro, in human language – Woman of Light, died several winters ago, and he buried her in an old abandoned hole where hares used to live, not far from his bush.

He often visited his beloved, sharing his thoughts, remembering the years they lived together and their children, whom fate scattered throughout the forest. In his youth, he worked hard, providing for her and her offspring making sure they had everything they needed. The children grew up and left home, but new ones were born, and the carousel of life kept spinning…

Then, suddenly, the time came when the children left their parents' home, and new ones were not born. That's when Khryukhryu and Khrokhro realized that old age had come. They continued to tenderly care for each other, but the years took their toll. One cold winter evening, she quietly went to Paradise, the one that was in Heaven, next to the Human Paradise. Khryukhryu felt, deep in his gut, that his beloved was happy there in Heaven and that she was waiting for him, but not in a hurry.

The time would come, and they would be together again, but in not a moment before God called. Now, he lived completely alone and crawled out of the hole only to clean his prickly fur coat, collect mushrooms and berries that fell from the bushes, and fresh grass for the bedding. About a kilometer from his home, on the edge of the forest, grew a lonely apple tree.

Oh, how he loved apples! Occasionally, gathering all his strength, he would set off on a journey – one that now felt long and difficult. If he was lucky, he would bring back a couple of fallen apples on his back - already rotting apples and, stretching out the pleasure, he would eat a small piece of this delight over a week or two. But everything comes to an end.

Once, during a hike to the edge of the forest, a fox blocked his path - he had to run away. He did run away, but he badly injured his back paw and, with great difficulty, having reached his home, he began to lick the wound and did not come out of the hole for about a week. Thank God, the paw healed, but he had to forget about trips to the apple tree for a while, and maybe forever.

God! How he loved these hikes! And not only because of the apples, but also because beyond the edge of the forest there was a field beyond which the city began. Don't be surprised,

Piglet loved this City, where in his distant youth he lived among people for a whole winter. He was young and inexperienced then, and so he fell into a trap. In the apartment where he was brought, four people lived: Dad, Mom, Son and Daughter.

They settled him near the sofa on which the boy slept, but Piglet stole an old newspaper and made himself a dwelling behind the sofa by the wall. Of course, this place was not as cozy as his parents' hole in the forest, but it was dry and warm here, and at night no one hunted him: not a fox, not an owl - this was the peace one could only dream of. He did not need to get food for himself.

They fed him all sorts of things and gave him water and milk to drink. He liked some of the food and some he didn't, but he ate it all, out of politeness. The water they gave him was too clean and tasteless, but he loved milk and drank the bowl right away, as if letting people know this is very tasty, please pour more.

One late autumn evening, Papa brought a sack of potatoes and a large wooden suitcase of apples from the village — a supply for the winter. He had never tried either one. The potatoes did not impress the hedgehog at all, but the apples.

My God, what a taste! Simply manna from heaven! Even the juiciest raspberries or porcini mushrooms did not compare to this delicacy. Khryukhryu gobbled up a piece of apple and grunted funny, like a toy pig. He fell in love with apples for the rest of his life. But you can't get full of delight, and a plan immediately ripened in his head. The suitcase with apples stood under Daughter's crib and was slightly ajar.

That same night, when the children fell asleep, he began Operation Times. All night long, he impaled the juicy fruits on needles and dragged them from the suitcase behind the sofa. By morning, his home was filled with wonderful yellow-green fruits, which had noticeably diminished in the suitcase.

Of course, in the morning, Mom noticed the loss of the "vitamins" and quickly discovered Khryukhryu's warehouse. The Son was ordered to immediately restore justice and put the apples back in the suitcase, which he did, leaving the largest and most beautiful apple behind the sofa. All winter long, the son, daughter and Khryukhryu received these wonderful fruits for dessert.

As people say, "Not life, but raspberries." But why raspberries and not apples? Spring has come. One Sunday, the father sat the son opposite him and said that the hedgehog should live in the forest to start his own family. As bitter as it was for the son, he took the prickly lump to the edge of the forest and let it go. Running behind an apple tree that grew at the edge of the field, Khryukhryu watched the boy, and he sat on the grass for a long time with tears running down his cheeks.

It was getting dark, the boy stood up, wiped his eyes with the sleeve of his shirt and slowly trudged towards the city. Farewell, my son and my friend – thought Khryukhryu and trotted off to his hole. The old hedgehog's heart ached from the memories. Old age is not scary – loneliness is scary. Evening rolled in, and then night. Khryukhryu ate a piece of mushroom and curled up for the night. Sleep did not come.

He tossed and turned and thought, thought, thought. He fell asleep only in the morning. He dreamed of Khryukhryu and the warm summer evening that they whiled away together under a spreading bush near their cozy hole, straightening each other's needles on their backs. The morning light interrupted the wonderful dream. He stuck his head out of his shelter and saw white flies falling from the sky to the ground. The first snow.

My God, he thought, another winter has come: an uncomfortable time and often hungry. The hedgehog crawled outside, cleaned his fur coat and, having gathered some fresh grass from under the bush, carried it to his hole and spread it over the old one, so that his old bones would lie softer. It was November, but the air already smelled of winter.

It was a bit early, he thought, well, whatever can be, but to his great pleasure the air warmed up in the morning. His wounded leg did not ache, which meant that it would be dry and warm for another week. What joy! "Tomorrow, early in the morning, I will try to get to the apple tree," he decided, "and maybe I will bring two or three apples for the winter."

In the morning, the sun was shining brightly and Khryukhryu decided to go to the treasured tree. He walked slowly, looking around every now and then, checking whether the fox was watching him. Of course, he knew that foxes hunted at night, and he himself was a night dweller, but he was still wary of the cunning danger. That's why he set out on a journey in the morning - foxes sleep during the day.

Khryukhryu took twice as long as usual to get to the apple tree, but as a reward for his efforts, he found a pile of fallen fruit beneath the tree - there was plenty to choose from. Happiness had arrived at last! Suddenly, a gang of boys ran up to the oak tree next to the apple tree.

The hedgehog tried to quickly hide and crawled under a nearby bush. But, as they say, "even an old woman can make a mistake" —he did not notice the boy hiding there, and in an instant, he found himself in the rascal's bag. "That's the end," he thought. The bag closed and darkness fell.

The door slammed. The bag was carefully placed on the floor and opened. The light from the light bulb under the ceiling hits his eyes. He slowly and cautiously crawled out of his captivity and found himself on the floor in the hallway. But what was this? Piglet would recognize this smell from hundreds of others. It was the apartment where he spent the "apple winter" in his distant youth. A boy leaned over him, very similar to the owner of the old sofa, and a tall man came out of the room, smelling like the son, once upon a time.

The old hedgehog understood everything at once: the son had now become the father, who had his own Son. Khryukhryu hobbled into the bedroom, the door to which was open. Seeing the old sofa, behind which once lay his home – he almost fainted. And when he saw a huge wooden suitcase full of apples behind the closet, he thought that he had finally lost his mind.

The Father, who had once been the son, shouted something and a woman unknown to him came from the kitchen, bent down and put a bowl of milk on the floor in front of Khryukhryu, and next to it she put a juicy yellow-green apple on an old newspaper.

Everything returned to normal, just like in his distant youth. People have nursing homes, and he found himself in the anteroom of Paradise. Khryukhryu lived behind the old sofa in warmth and prosperity for two winters. The hedgehog passed away peacefully in his sleep at the very end of the second winter. At the gates of Paradise, his beloved Khrokhro was already waiting for him. Happiness will never leave you if you are a good person or. a hedgehog.

Lechaim
(To Life)

Hello! My name is Chubby. I am old and sick with a bunch of diseases, but in my soul - I am a young pup. All my adult life, I wanted to share my memories, but somehow, I never dared. And honestly, there was no one to share them with. Who is interested in the emotional outpourings of a dog? Now, feeling that my life has reached the home stretch, I've finally decided to take this step. Here, I turn on the recorder listen – if, of course, someone will ever hear me.

I was born on the twenty-eighth of April, nineteen ninety-four (My God! In the last century!) in New York City.

Together with me, four brothers were born, the same as me, black in color, and one, red-colored, sister. My father had a fierce character. He hated everyone and everything, considering himself the master of the area, which is impossible to do here on Staten Island, the fiefdom of the mafia: here every master has his own boss.

So, they put my future daddy on a chain, but one day he broke free, attacked a young dog, did his dirty deed and rushed after a car that he didn't like for some reason. The result was a broken hind leg. From that day on, he remained a lame, chained dog for the rest of his days. But my mother remained the standard of kindness all her life. She reminded me of a shy schoolgirl of the late nineteenth century, devoting herself to her children and caring for her crippled, good-for-nothing husband. You might be interested in how I know all this about my parents.

Ah, it's very simple: at night, when the windows are open in the summer, you can often hear dogs barking and cats meowing - this is our Internet. We are animals – we communicate with our brains and voices, not with our fingers and buttons, like you humans.

There was a tragedy in the family of my future Master: at a fairly young age, Gerd, my pre-trainer, died of a heart attack on June 8, 1994. The next day, an ad appeared in the local newspaper about the sale of puppies, that is, about me and my brothers and sister. The next evening, a family of three appeared in our house: mom, dad and him- my future Master. We were let out into the room onto the carpet and at that very moment his eyes met mine.

We instantly made our choice. I ran (if it could be called a run) to the young guy, chewed the lace of his shoe and licked the toe of his shoe. It was a mark that meant - I'm yours! My future Master pulled a bottle of white nail polish out of my mother's purse and dabbed it on the tip of my already trimmed tail. People are strange creatures!

Why did he do that? I would have recognized him in a million – even without any scents or markings. I was supposed to be picked up in three weeks, but we could no longer exist without each other. Just one week later, having licked my mother's nose, I left the place of my birth and went by car to his house.

And so, allow me to introduce myself once again. My full name, registered in the state of New York, is Lord Chubs, I am a Doberman Pinscher. As is customary for our appearance, my tail had already trimmed, but my ears still had to be dealt with. For us Dobermans, ear trimming is something like a tooth extraction for a person.

The procedure, to put it mildly, is creepy, but there's no way around it. I have to look like an "evil beauty". But how am I supposed to look intimidating when I'm barely twenty-five centimeters long (or one foot, if you prefer the English system of measurements) and my voice is more reminiscent of a hoarse mouse than the Scarecrow from Andersen's fairy tale "Tinderbox". And now, the most important thing: when I entered (or rather was carried) into my new house, the very first thing I noticed was the smell. This house smelled of love and kindness. Of course, I am not a slug and did not want to be born a lapdog. I am a Doberman. and suddenly such a feeling?!

Not finding an answer, I put off discussing this issue for later. In the meantime, I was standing on the rug near the closet with the door slightly open, from which a delicious smell of used shoes came. Without thinking twice, I stuck my nose into the crack and, grabbing the first shoe I came across, pulled it out.

This shoe turned out to be the slipper of the Master's mother. I licked the heel of that shoe and my head spun with pleasure. My God, what a tzimmes (a delight - where did I learn this Hebrew word from?). But then I immediately realized that I would be punished for what I had done. So, biting the toe of the slipper gently, I sat down on the side of my bottom and, tilting my head to the left, looked at the woman.

To my surprise, she said to her son: "Lev, let him chew on this old slipper, it's all torn anyway, and I have a new pair." That's how I learned that my boss's name was Lev, but for me he would remain the Boss for the rest of my life. Lev's father, a huge guy almost as tall as the ceiling, stood to the side and smiled at something.

That's when I truly felt that I would be well and warm in this house, which was now mine too. I was right - the house smelled of happiness, comfort, well, and a little bit of a delicious smell of cutlets wafted from the kitchen.

While people were looking on with affection as I gnawed on an old slipper, which, frankly speaking, I was already quite tired of, I thought to myself that I had had enough of fiddling with shoes and, throwing the slipper aside, I went to the stairs leading to the second floor. Let me explain - for you, humans, only five minutes of my fiddling with the slipper had passed, but for me, in my dog's time, a whole thirty-five minutes had passed! Got it? And so – I was at the stairs. In general, for us Dobermans, stairs are a stumbling block, but that's when my dad's character kicked in: fearless of anything and anyone (unfortunately, not out of great intelligence). I sniffed the air - it carried the scent of the place where people sleep. Without hesitation, I fearlessly began climbing the steps. Thank God they were covered with carpet; my claws could grip the surface. If not for that, my ascent would have been ruined.

Having reached the second floor, I turned my muzzle (alas, dogs have no face, only muzzles - and this is extremely sad) and, standing in the pose of a mountain goat, stared at the residents of the house. The owner and his parents looked at me in surprise, not understanding how I dared to climb the stairs to the second floor, because we, Dobermans, are afraid of this "exercise" as if it were fire. But while they stood with their mouths open in surprise, I went to inspect, as I thought, my future possessions.

There was no room for me in the small bedroom; in the Owner's room, in addition to furniture, the floor was strewn with clothes, books, shoes and other junk, which prevented me from even entering it, let alone finding a place for myself. But in the bedroom of Lev's parents, I immediately chose a corner for myself by the door: it was cozy here and until midday the sun's rays would warm my, as I thought, future home.

On top of that, there was a nice smell of clean bed linen and there were two toilets nearby – one for people and one for me, where I would drink water from the toilet when, as you can imagine, I grew up. Lost in my dreams, I curled up in "my corner" and dozed off. I was torn away from such pleasant thoughts by the loud slap of a rolled-up newspaper on my palm.

The Master was standing next to me. He hit my palm with the bundle again and said just as sharply: "You can't! Your place!" – and walked towards the stairs, looking me sternly in the eyes. I pretended not to understand what they wanted from me, but no such luck, the Master grabbed my collar with his fingers and pulled me along. We are Dobermans, smart creatures and I, realizing that I had lost, hobbled towards the stairs.

Lyova let me go ahead and commanded: "Down!" Here my problems began: going down turned out to be much more difficult than climbing up. Sideways, on my bottom, I somehow slid down to the middle of the stairs and. stopped –

I suddenly became scared. The owner, as if teasing me, easily ran down the steps and beckoned with his finger, like come on, come on, don't waste time.

I forced myself to pull it together, took a step down —and promptly lost my balance, sliding down on my belly right to Lev's feet. I grabbed his slipper, did a somersault, and landed belly up near the closet. The humans laughed until they cried at my "circus act", and I felt so ashamed - not like a formidable Doberman, but more like a clumsy kitten. Luckily, my owner defused the situation. He said: "Chubby, let's go, I'll show you your real place," and led me to the kitchen.

I can't say that I was delighted with my new place of residence, which was wedged between the glass door to the terrace and the gas stove. Sure, it was warm there, and the sun hit just right until about one o'clock in the afternoon. And yes, it smelled delicious of food. But still, this place was far from the Master's room, and that made me feel pretty lonely. Why do people choose their houses and furniture to their taste, but we - dogs - have to live where we are ordered? Wait — stop! I am a dog and must obey humans! Who came up with this nastiness — this unfair rule? People say that God punished me this way. Who is this God? I don't know any God! Never met him! But the Master said this is my place, so I guess this will be my corner.

That's it! I decided - so it shall be! Tired of all this worry, I curled up on the mat that Lev brought and sweetly (as people would say) dozed off, covering my nose with my paw. You people, when you get married, take a long time to "get used to" each other. Well, it's the same goes for us dogs —except we need to get used not to our own kind, but to you - people. It is rare when dog owners have the desire to "get used to" the animal. In this sense, I was very lucky: both the Owner, and his mother, and even this Big Man tried to find a connection with me from the first day of my stay in the house. I even got the impression that they often forgot who they were dealing with and cooed at me like I was a kitten, and I am a Doberman.

The first night in the new place was restless: I couldn't fall asleep for a long time, and when I fell asleep, I dreamed of my mother and, waking up, I whined loudly, giving the inhabitants of the house no peace. I wished I would grow up already, stop whining and… peeing on the bedding. I felt ashamed and even blushed from these thoughts, but people, unfortunately, do not see how dogs blush.

Or maybe it's for the best. On the second day, bright and early in the morning, I went to school. No, of course, not like children go to school; my Master began to teach me the rules of good etiquette. In other words, he began to teach me how to sit, how to lie down, how to walk, how and when to eat and drink, how and when to relieve myself, and so on, and so forth. He repeated orders two or even three times, and this often offended me.

We dog, especially Dobermans, are very smart creatures. I don't need a command repeated several times – one look into my eyes and you'll immediately see that I understand everything. Sometimes, though, I just don't want to obey, but want to fool around and play, because our life is seven times shorter than yours, humans. Oh, and one more thing: we don't need a Universal Translator, like in the TV series "Star Trek". We understand all languages, because the most important thing is not what you tell us, but how you do it.

So, when you humans reach this elementary simple truth, then all the problems between you and us end. Well, my training began with where I can urinate and relieve myself. Lyova fenced off a section of the kitchen measuring one meter by one meter, covered it with newspapers and said: "Here you can relieve yourself." I would like to point out that in my opinion, given the crap that is printed in the press, the newspapers were used for their intended purpose.

So, I tilted my head slightly to the side and looked up at the Master, as if to ask, "Do you want me to pee on the floor covered with newspaper?" - and, not seeing any denial in his gaze, I took a big piss on the portrait of the Governor of New York. We Dobermans have never been, and never will be, liberals. This is our political credo, if you will.

Why do cats get special trays with sand to relieve themselves, and we have to start with a newspaper on the floor? Absurd! Nevertheless, I politely walked over to the fence and lay down next to it, humming to myself the words of a song from the funny old film - ". normal heroes always go around." We dogs do not sleep all night long but wake up from every rustle. And therefore, we think a lot "about life" in the silence of the night.

My predecessor, Gerd, often communicates with me from our dog paradise. Yes, there is such a place as an animal paradise, but you humans may not understand this. Gerd lived a very short life, but a life full of love and peace. Gerd ushka, as the Mountain Man called him, was a dog of rare beauty and intelligence.

The huge man, whom the Master calls dad, called Gerd an intellectual. He often said that Gerd should have lived in Buckingham Palace, spending his days lounging by the fireplace with one paw elegantly bent at the knee, and in the evenings contemplating the royal family as they discussed world affairs over glasses of port. But fate had other plans. Gerd lived his life in New York, in a family of emigrants from the Soviet Union, but he did not regret it for a second.

Lev's dad is a very gentle person by nature, but he is so big that calling him dad is somehow strange, the word father suits him better. Perhaps that is why my Master calls him softly "Papa". So, Man-Mount christened me Lomonosov, adding with a grin that I was a rural, uncouth, but very clever boor.

The head of this family always has his own opinion on various matters, which are not accepted by family members and friends. Sometimes, they even laugh at him behind his back, simply considering him an idiot. But still –he is a man who has his own opinion. And that, in itself, is already worth something. Oh, and yes – I should not forget to ask Gerd who this Lomonosov fellow is. My parents never mentioned this name.

Please understand that I came from the house of commoners to the abode of educated people. Just listen to how I speak now! Wow!

Something is hurting me, I'll go lie down on the terrace and warm it in the sun –it helps us dogs better than headache medicine for people. Huh? What? Where am I? Ah, here I am, awake.

The sun has already gone to the other side of the house; my headache has gone. How long did I sleep? Almost two hours, wow! Yes, I have aged greatly. Well, okay, what's the point of judging and arguing, I'll continue dictating my memories. I'm turning on the recorder, well, let's go.

And so, my Master began my education with the ability to urinate and everything else – on the newspaper. Every day, the area of the floor covered with fresh newsprint grew smaller, and I tried my best to relieve myself in the middle of the "Firing Zone". It reminded me of parachutists making careful, drawn-out jumps in order to land exactly in the center of the circle.

The only difference was that the parachutists controlled the canopy with their hands so that their feet landed precisely on the target, while I had to control my entire body so that the stream from my manhood hit the portrait of the governor or even the president himself. Well. and then came the day when Lev took me outside for the first time.

My God! How many new smells! I had to try to remember them all and mark the places of our canine communication, but I did not have that much urine. Here's your first lesson, Chubby: you need to drink more and hold on longer to leave a message to new acquaintances like "a Doberman Pinscher named Lord Chubs walked here, please keep this in mind."

Due to the lack of fluid, I had to lie on the grass and rub myself to leave my scent, which the Master was very unhappy about and sharply warned me: "Chubby, be careful - ticks!" Yes, I know all about these "cute bugs" from Mom and Dad. In response, I barked, which meant: "I won't do it again" - and we went home. A few weeks passed, and we went to a sadistic dog doctor who cropped ears.

Yes, such is our Doberman fate – ears that droop from birth is supposed to be high, straight, and sharp-tipped, standing proudly. To achieve this, they must be cropped. Now I just remember it - and it hurts. As soon as we entered the inquisitor's reception room, I saw one of my brothers and my sister. There was a lot of joyful fussing under the chairs where our Masters were sitting.

My brother, although a chatterbox, is extremely shy by nature. My sister, on the other hand, is a red-haired beauty with a rather unsociable character: I told her: "You don't need to get married - you're ready to become a mother-in-law right away."

Actually, we Dobermans have no right to be afraid of anything, but the uncertainty of the upcoming procedure excited me to such an extent that I ended up peeing under the Master's chair. "Here's a woman and St. George's Day for you!" - an old Russian proverb. And where did I know it from? Most likely, it was hereditary information; one of my ancestors must have lived in Russia. My philosophical thoughts were interrupted by the nurse's voice: "Lord Chubs, please come into the office." Dark circles swam before my eyes and I, swaying slowly, walked into the inquisition room.

I don't remember anything else, or rather, I don't want to remember. I woke up in a room next to the operating room; a strange construction of metal and bandages towered over my head, and a collar was on my neck, similar to those worn by the English queen and ladies of the court in the sixteenth century. Seeing my reflection in the mirror, I shook with horror that not only my ears had been cut off, but also my manhood. But after sniffing myself and finding no changes in the stomach area, I calmed down a little.

I don't want to say anything more about the four weeks of torment with the Leaning Tower of Pisa on my head (you understand that my four weeks felt like your six months), but I will only say this: I hated the surgeon who did the "circumcision" on me.

After they took off my "headdress" and collar, my ears looked great - now I'm a full-fledged Doberman! People on the street, when I went for a walk, paid attention to my exterior and nodded their heads approvingly, and at home, in revenge on my tormentor-surgeon, I sometimes bent one ear, as if to say to the doctor: "Look at your work, schlimazl, and don't be too flattered by the result!" As if he could see or hear me. Among us, experts in literature, this is called "showing a fig in your pocket." Just think, I'm already an expert in literature!

As the Man-Mount said: "He's so smart because he lives across from the school, and his mind just falls off in pieces." Time went on, I grew, mastering the lessons the residents of our house kept feeding me. Oh, it's already our house, and look, I'll soon consider myself one of the owners of this dwelling. Look at that!

I lived in a society of conservative Republicans, so of course I couldn't have a liberal outlook on life. Still, sometimes I was irritated by certain situations. For example, the Mountain Man often watched the evening news on CNN –a low-brow liberal TV channel, as he said - because it helped him understand the ideology of the enemy. Or here's another joke: my Master insistently demanded that

I walk on his left side whenever he gives the command "heel". Well, what if I'm left-pawed? They don't make you write with your right hand at school if you feel more comfortable doing everything with your left. Luckily for me, I'm right-pawed anyway, but as the actor Pavel Luspekaev said in the film "White Sun of the Desert": "It's a shame for the country".

A wonderful film - the horses play superbly in it. According to statistics, twenty percent of Dobermans are left-handed, so how do they cope with these costs of a Democratic Dictatorship. As for me, I walked on the left side of the Master with my head held high, chest forward, ears up – nature had not shortchanged me in stature. When I was nine months old, I began to notice that passersby walking along the sidewalk towards us began to cross to the opposite side of the street.

Why was that? Probably because people were afraid of the Mountain Man, who walked with me in the evenings more often than anyone else. I no longer squatted under a bush to leave a message "written" by me for my friends but would dashingly lift my hind leg and leave my autograph on tree trunks. Once, on New Year's Eve, Mama-Galya, coming to the window, said to my Master: "Look outside, how much snow is falling."

I knew nothing about snow yet and saw it for the first time. Huge flakes of something white, like pieces of cotton wool, were falling from the sky, pouring out of my sleeping couch, which they bought me instead of bedding, when I managed to tear it.

We Dobermans love to chew and tear rags: I, for example, love to chew, bite and pull threads from a piece of thick rope that the Master gave me. It was getting dark quickly outside - it was time for my lunch. I went to the kitchen and approached my table to remind Galya about my empty stomach. Yes, I had my own dining table with two bowls: one for food and one for water. Having eaten half of my portion, I went to the corner and lay down on my couch. For some reason, I felt sad and lost my appetite.

The Master wasn't home - he had run off to his friends to celebrate the New Year, completely forgetting about me. I don't need champagne, but good company, like my Master, wouldn't hurt. Quite a prospect for me, I tell you, to celebrate such a holiday with old people. I was in a bad mood and decided to spoil the evening for the Man-Mount: I went up to the armchair in which he was sitting, stare at the TV screen, sat down opposite him and started whining. He immediately understood that I needed to go outside to relieve myself.

Cursing, he reluctantly got up from the armchair and went to put on his jacket and shoe covers for a walk. I obediently offered him my neck with the collar, and he deftly fastened the leash before opening the front door. What happened next, I am ashamed to remember, but I have to tell it.

The front door opened, and I saw and smelled the snow. It was no longer falling from the sky but lying on the ground – forty centimeters of this muck in just a couple of hours. I had to break my way to the street with my chest, like a bulldozer pushing through a blade of ice. I fought with this disgrace for ten long minutes until I finally reached the first tree to leave my mark on it. I raised my hind leg this way and that, in order to convey the correct message to the neighbors about my health and mood –and, of course, to congratulate them on the New Year. But my handwriting was very uneven with many mistakes.

I immediately remembered a joke that I recently heard from Borya, The Mountain Man: "One morning under the windows of the Louvre in the snow was written in urine "The King is a fool". His Majesty called the chief detective and ordered him to find out who did it. In the evening of the same day, the investigator informed the King that according to the urine analysis, it was the German ambassador, and according to the handwriting - the Queen." Ha!

It is difficult for you humans to understand, but you should try to leave a proper mark on a tree when your, so to speak, "male dignity" is lowered into cold wet snow. Remember how you enter the cold water of the sea to swim, and a wave suddenly covers you from your knees to your waist? Well, this is child's play compared to what I experienced when leaving an autograph on a tree trunk. My first acquaintance with snow had a strong effect on my psyche and all that...

I hated it, and since that day, every walk in the "white kingdom", as some classic one called it, gave me a headache – and not just that. And yet, this New Year's Eve unexpectedly brought me joy. Excuse me, but these memories have tired me out a little. I must take a nap, but I will continue my story a little later.

New Year's Eve has arrived. There were three of us in the house: Mama Galya, the Mountain Man, and your humble servant. I want to note that Galya is an excellent cook – how do I know? Two reasons: my Master's belly is growing by leaps and bounds, and I start salivating profusely whenever Mama goes into the kitchen.

That night, the table was set with such delicacies that when Galya and Borya sat down to see out the Old Year, my head started spinning. Swaying and nearly fainting from hunger, I wandered to my little sofa and collapsed. My own table was also set: one bowl filled with dog food, another with fresh water, and between them lay a tasty bone.

But sniffing Mama's delicacies and eating something from my table was beyond my strength. I laid my head on my paws and tried to fall asleep, when suddenly the Mountain Man called me. "What else?" I thought, reluctantly getting up, and went to the dining room, like a well-drilled soldier on the order of the sergeant major to take up duty. Borya called me over and ordered me to sit down, which I did, expressing with my eyes the deepest degree of sadness of which I was capable.

And suddenly! "Three Yards Up" (that's what I called Galya's husband behind his back because of his enormous height), brought a fork with a piece of deliciously smelling meat to my nose and said: "Chubby, you can take this, but very carefully, intelligently." I gently took a piece of tasty treat with my front teeth, chewed and swallowed, swooning with pleasure, while a new piece of cutlet was already looming on his fork. From that moment, I realized that Borya is a very kind man, but so big that dogs and small children, whom he loves tenderly, are a little afraid of him. We dog, are used to looking up at people from knee height, but such tall men cause us certain inconveniences: it is easier to look at them from a distance, like Elbrus in the clouds from a neighboring city. Yet, when commanded to stay close, we must be in close proximity to a person and this requires great dedication from us, trained dogs.

If you had seen me at that moment, you would have understood that Borya and I have become very close friends since that New Year's Eve. By our dog standards, my belly is now as big as the belly of the Mountain Man. I grew up, studied and… continued to receive tasty morsels from Galya and Borya's table, of course, when the Master wasn't looking. Lyova was very angry about this, and Borya explained it very simply - he, Chubby, is a member of our family and deserves a treat from the table when he behaves well.

Of course, I supported Mountain Man's point of view; it was incredibly difficult to resist gobbling up something from the table. I assure you that you wouldn't be able to resist either, knowing how Galya cooks.

In March of 1996, my Master got married and moved out of his father's house into a separate apartment. "Oh, woe is me!" – as one thousand years old Genie Hottabych would say. But as the old saying goes, every cloud has a silver lining: they began to teach me less, and I began to get more from the table.

My main Mistress, in my opinion, now became Galya. She suited me better in character: we are both lively and do not like to sit in one place for a long time, and most importantly - she cooks food! Now, don't get me wrong – I didn't start respecting Borya any less. Well, maybe just a little... but he doesn't need to know about that. You see, we Dobermans are very smart creatures, and it was easier for me to find a common language with Galya. For Borya, receiving tasty and plentiful food was a common thing, but for me it was like manna from heaven. I could do something naughty, for which Galya punished me, but she would quickly soften and give me a piece of a treat or, at worst, dog candy.

It was more difficult with Borya: even when he took me out for a walk, I had to walk on the left on a short leash on the command "heel." God forbid I jerked left or right – his left hand would lift my front half of my body into the air like a crane. I would hang there, losing the support of my front paws, looking like some kind of cur. It was useless to resist, Mountain Man was a strong guy and I made the only sensible decision at that moment – to obey the command. When we reached the walking spot, he would let me off the leash, and just as I settled down to leave my "message", he'd slip a plastic bag under my butt and all my "newspaper news" would fall right into it.

Borya was happy – he didn't have to clean up after me. The trouble was that because of this "lethal risk act", as they say in the circus, the animal world around me knew very little about me, and dogs and cats considered me some kind of incognito show-off who didn't want to communicate with anyone. Sad.

And yet, I had one outlet - playing with a tennis ball on a basketball court. This court was surrounded by a tall mesh fence with a locking gate. We would come to the court when there was no one there; Borya would close the gate, throw the ball into the far corner, and I'd sprint around like a maniac, dragging the ball back to the Mountain Man. I'd sit down beside him, tongue hanging out, eyes fixed on his hand – waiting to see where he'd throw this magic toy next. The moment I caught its direction, I'd race off to find it, grab it with my teeth, and drag it back to the bench where Borya sat.

We played this wonderful game for about twenty minutes, after which we slowly walked home, where I, having caught my breath, drank a whole bowl of cold fresh water and collapsed on the carpet to take a little nap, thinking that life was one big pleasure. The owner and his wife occasionally visited our house, and I, forgetting everything in the world – including my mother's delicacies, rubbed myself against his feet. When he took me for a walk, I followed all his commands, eager to show what I had learned, secretly hoping that he would take me with him to his new home and we would live together again.

I was even ready to switch completely to a dog diet. But that wasn't destined to happen: Lev got a new job and moved with his wife, Elya, to Florida. Since then, I've only received news about the Master's family from Galya and Borya, who visited him when he and his family lived in Jacksonville.

I saw Lev's two children for the first time when they moved to live in New Jersey. We met rather rarely; Levand Elya were busy with their family and work – so the few hours I spent with them were the happiest times for me. I tried my best not to show how much I missed the Master, but I was not very successful. Lev's ancestors, sensing the state of my soul, gave me all their love and treated me as a fully-fledged member of their family.

As far as I know, few of my dog and cat friends lived as sweetly and comfortably as I have. I especially feel this now, as I grow older and sense that my life is coming to an end. We animals feel the proximity of departure to the Other World much more acutely than people.

My dear Master!

I know that after I leave, sooner or later, you will bring a dog into your home— and it will definitely be a Doberman Pinscher. I am sure that his life will be long and sweet because you will give him all the love you couldn't give me. You had other, more important things to do - believe me, I understand that well, for I know it from the two people who cared for me and loved me. But I still remember the smell and taste of your shoelace, which I gently chewed when we chose each other: you, choosing me as your dog, and I, choosing you as my Master.

Well, that seems to be it.

Your Chabbi.

Stop the recorder.

An Unusual Ordinary Fairy Tale

(AN OLD STORY IN A NEW WAY)

This happened in ancient times, long forgotten by people. That is why stories from ancient times are called fairy tales. Yet, our people need to remember what happened in those grays, forgotten times. Now, when they hear these tales, they dismiss them with a wave of their hands and a shake of their heads, saying it couldn't have happened – that it's always been that way. But the truth faded from people's memory because the Church said it was not the work of God, and therefore it could not have happened.

Well, people have forgotten the deeds of those ancient years. But there were a few people who passed on this tale from mouth to mouth, from immemorial times sunk into oblivion. So, gather around, sit in a circle, and listen to the story that came from ancient times.

As my distant ancestors used to say, there once lived three heroes in Rus'. The eldest was named Dobrynya Nikitich. He was born in the Russian land, though his father came to Rus' from a distant land - Israel. Dobrynya was wise and strong, well-versed in many things, but quiet by nature - not one to boast.

The middle one was named Ilya Muromets. It was said that he sat idle until he was thirty, Storytellers claimed it was because there was prosperity in his parents' house. And Ilyusha himself was very lazy, lazier than a fat cat that always sleeps on the stove. So, when the prosperity in the house dried up, and his parents fell ill, and he himself began to grow thin, he finally realized that this path could lead to death.

Then Ilya rose from the bench to his full heroic height, stretched, and went out into the world – wherever his eyes looked, forgetting about his parents, simply saddled his horse and took some food for the road. Whether he walked for a long time or a short time is unknown to us. He wandered through the forest, like a lost soul – until one day, Hemet Dobrynya in some woods.

Toward evening, they lit a fire and roasted a couple of hares, ate, washed it down with honey, and began a slow, simple conversation: where are you from, and where are you going, and what are your wishes? They talked and chatted for a while and fell asleep under the full moon by a small river on the soft grass that smelled of mint.

In the morning, they woke up with the first rays of the sun, got ready, bathed in the river and sat down under a spreading tree to eat bread and milk. Then, Ilyusha turned to Dobrynya and said, "Let's perform some kind of military feat or free someone from captivity. They say that the Dragon has dragged Varvara-Beauty to his castle and will have a wedding against her will.

Dobrynya, let's go to that castle and chop off all three of Gorynych's heads, so that he won't dare steal our girls." To which Dobrynya replies: "You, Ilyushenka, seem like a village fool, you're talking utter nonsense. Have you seen that Serpent? No. Oh, I've met him more than once.

That Dragon is the size of a thousand-year-old oak, and when he spreads his wings, he covers half the field. Sometimes he steals a dozen cows for dinner - that's his idea of robbery. Well, tell me, my friend Muromets, what is he supposed to do with that Varvara? Just play with dolls.

That snake is looking for a female of his kind to bear him children. And as for you saying he stole Varvara! Pfft, people are babbling outrageous lies just to wag their tongues, that Varvara lives with Baba Yaga – she runs a fun establishment for the peasants. "

Then Ilya said, "You, Dobrynya Nikitich, know so many things –, your mind is not ours - not Russian. And though you are of Jewish blood, as people say, I respect you very much. Tell me Nikitich, do you know how far away Baba Yaga's house is?"

"Why, of course," replied Dobrynya. " It will take three days to get through the dense forest, if you go straight."

Ilya jumped into the saddle, reared his horse, and shouted that it had been a long time since he had squeezed a woman, so why shouldn't the two of them visit that cheerful house?

The heroes agreed and set off through that dreadful dense forest, through deep ravines and high hills. They slept under the moon and rose with the sun. They ate right in the saddles, so as not to waste time. On the third day of the journey, at noon, they rode out into a clearing, unsaddled their horses and lay down in the shade to rest a little before the evening festivities. Suddenly, through their sleep, they heard the sound of horses' hooves. Rubbing their eyes, they saw a young hero riding a horse of a curious color, with a pink saddle. The handle of his sword is decorated with intricate monograms, and the bow, where the bowstring was attached, was adorned with various trinkets. The young man himself was handsome with a ribbon mustache and a wedge-shaped beard, full reddish lips, and a rosy blush on his cheeks. The horse's mane was braided and decorated with beads. Both the rider and the horse looked ahead with a mysterious, languid gaze.

The young man jumped down from the saddle and introduced himself, bowing in a non-Russian manner. "My name is Alyosha Popovich, and I am on my way from the

Greeks to the Varangians. I left my father's house in Grekovia a year ago. I am traveling through different lands to see the world and meet different people." Then our knights invited Alexei to join them on their way to the Merry House, where Baba Yaga is said to be the mistress.

The young man happily agreed, slipped his feet into his Moroccan boots, and placed them in the stirrups. Then, in a quiet voice, he said, - "Don't call me Alexei, heroes, but call me Alyosha." Dobrynya and Ilya agreed: you were given a name, so it's up to you to decide what you want to be called. The sun clung to the tops of the trees, signaling that evening was near. The knights jumped into their springy saddles and set their stagnant horses into a gallop.

Their helmets and swords were shining, their leather armor was decorated with silver, and their bows and arrows looked menacing in their quivers. The horses' manes flapped in the wind, the earth flew up beneath their hooves, and steam rose from the horses' nostrils as they galloped. The forest creatures and birds were quiet - three heroes were riding to the Merry House for a journey.

The sun was setting behind the horizon. The young men stopped on a hillock, covered their eyes from the sun with their palms. Nearby in a clearing, stood a hut on chicken legs, smoke coming out of the chimney and carrying the delicious scent of mash The riders rode up to the hut when it was already dark. The birds fell silent, and only the trees rustled their leaves, as if quietly whispering about the arrival of guests.

It was so dark you could poke your eye out. All the forest creatures hid – it was scary, and that was all. Our knights jumped off their horses, holding their horses by the bridles and grinning – thinking about the night's revelry. Then Alyosha said: "Little hut, little hut, turn your front to the forest, and your back to me."

The hut squatted down awkwardly, unsure which way to turn, and then a whistle and noise from the sky – the mistress herself arrived in a mortar. The old witch Baba Yaga was still a young woman at that time, about a hundred and twenty years old, no more. She climbed out of the mortar briskly and, without haste, approached the heroes. She looked them over from head to toe and said: "Well, you are good kids, especially you," winking at Alyosha. He immediately blushed, whether from youth or something else. Then she leaned closely and whispered to him: "You obviously got it all wrong out of fear. Hut, hut, turn your back to the forest and your front to me. You have completely disgraced the old wreck."

The house groaned and turned as it should, the light in the window began to glow and everything in the clearing became visible. Then Ilyusha could not stand it and said: "In this kennel,

Yaga, there will hardly be enough room for you alone." And Yaga answered him: "Don't be afraid, Ilyusha, but go inside the door, and then you will see." The young men unsaddled their good horses, gave them some oats, and entered the hut.

They looked around in surprise, unable to grasp what had just happened: a large room opened before them with a tiled stove at the far wall, a table with benches, and carved stools decorated the room. Windows with shutters and wonderful frames, candles in carved candlesticks illuminated the room. It smelled deliciously of freshly baked bread and fresh milk. In the middle of the hall stood three beauties - Varvara the Beautiful Long Braid, Marya the Craftswoman, and Vasilisa the Wise. Each wore flowing silk sarafans and polished boots on their feet.

Each wore a kokoshnik with precious stones on her head - diamonds and sapphires, and their fingers were decorated with gold rings. The beauties gracefully bowed to the heroes from the waist and invited them to the table for dinner.

On that table, a multitude of homemade brews, honey, and various dishes were spread out. Baba Yaga, dressed in all black, sat at the head of the table, smiling warmly as she invited the knights to dine. The young heroes sat down at the table - Dobrynya with Maria, Ilya with Varvara, and Alyosha with Vasilisa. Baba Yaga watched her guests with delight, as she pondered something quietly to herself. The hostess clapped her hands and a couple of wood goblins jumped out from behind the stove and started playing music on their pipes. The guests drank and ate their fill and started dancing with the girls. Dobrynya with Marya and Ilyusha with Varvara were squirming, so hot that they were thrown into a fever. Baba Yaga herself started dancing around the mortar, and the cat was spinning from side to side on the stove and tapping his tail. Only Alyosha and Vasilisa were sitting near the stove, holding hands and quietly whispering about something.

The moon had risen - it was past midnight. The guests were a little tired. Baba Yaga clapped her hands, and the wood goblins disappeared as if they had never been, and the cat purred, stretched and fell asleep at once. Then the hostess said, "It's time, dear guests, to show your honor. If you love my maidens, go with them to the bedchambers, but only promise me that in the morning you will not leave until you hear my order."

The guests bowed to Yaga as a sign of consent and went to bed: Dobrynya with Marya, Ilya with Varvara, and Alyosha with Vasilisa. That night flew by quickly for the dear ones and it was sweeter than honey for Ilya and Dobrynya, and Alyosha and Vasilisa sat all night long holding hands and sharing secrets. At dawn, everyone went down to the room to eat bread and milk and listen to Baba Yaga's orders.

The hostess was silent while the guests were having breakfast. After a moment of thought, she said, "My good fellows, if you wish to marry my girls, then here is my command for you - go to the thrice-nine lands and the thirtieth kingdom, find my brother Koschei the Deathless and kill the damned bloodsucker. He, the villain, wants to take Vasilisa the Beautiful as his wife, but refuses to offer a worthy ransom. You and I, Yaga, are close relatives, so we will come to an agreement for thanks.

Well, I showed him the door - twice. Now he breathes malice against me, and I fear that the accursed robber will steal Vasilisa. So, heroes, here is my entire order." The heroes bowed to the mistress at the waist, took their damask swords, bows and sharp arrows, jumped into the saddles, put their feet in the stirrups and set their horses into a gallop, eager to reach the thirtieth kingdom to fight Koshchei.

They were in such a hurry that they forgot to kiss their betrothed on the lip's goodbye, but the trouble was, they could not return - doing so would be a bad omen, and the road would be lost to them forever. They galloped to the river and began searching for a ford. As soon as they found a crossing, someone called out to them from the bushes above the bank.

Evening twilight had already fallen when the three horsemen dismounted, and here in the light of the torches, they recognized Varvara, Marya and Vasilisa. They all sat down by the fire to have supper, and Varvara said: "It is not right for you to do such a task alone. We, your faithful friends, will be of use to you: we will feed you, give you something to drink, and put you to bed, so that you can do your work and not worry about anything else."

The knights dined with what God sent and went to bed, and the maidens tidied up the clearing by the river, watered the horses and gave them some food, and then they themselves went to bed next to their betrothed. Only Vasilisa and Alyosha sat on the grass leaning against a tree, holding hands and gazing at the starry sky, whispering about their own affairs. With the first rays of the sun, everyone was already in saddles, and having crossed the river, galloped off to the kingdom of Kashchei the Deathless.

Whether they rode for a long time or a short time, I don't know, but by nightfall they set up camp on a hillock from which Koshchei's Castle was visible. They ate and began to discuss how they would fight the monster. Ilya was the first to speak, saying that he had heard from his grandfather that Koshchei's death lay at the end of a needle; that needle was in an egg, the egg was inside a duck, the duck was inside a hare, the hare inside a chest that hung on a tall oak tree — and only Koshchei himself knew where that oak tree stood. His comrades listened to Ilyusha and became sad — where would they find that tree now? They couldn't ask Koshchei himself. And only Dobrynya Nikitich smiled into his mustache and said, "Your grandfather, Ilya, heard this tale from his grandfather, and he from his, and each time either a duck, or a hare, or an egg was added to this chatter.

I suppose it was on Easter when your grandfather was drunk that he told you this story. I'll tell you what, I saw a scripture in the great city of Jerusalem, where it was written in black and white, from right to left, that Kashchei was a prince who was bewitched because he wrote hooligan ditties against the Christian faith. Such a punishment was imposed on him that it was impossible to get rid of it.

Baba Yaga understood it too - after all, she is his own sister. That's why she does nasty things to people, so that everyone would hate her. Such a misfortune was imposed on the family of the Immortals, and that's why he is called the Kashchei the Immortal – that is his surname." Dobrynin's friends started making noise, waving their hands and saying, "You've completely lost your mind! You say you saw the writing from right to left, but you know that writing should be read from left to right."

"Well, you're a good man and you've gone too far. Remember when we drove up to a huge stone at the crossroads, with writing from left to right? It said: if you go

80

left, you'll lose your horse; if you go right, you'll lose your life. But you went straight ahead, and your forehead smashed against the stone with all you might. That must have really screwed up your brains! It was written from right to left! Ha! Ha! Ha!"

"Oh, I feel sorry for you, such fools," said Dobrynya. "What do you think all people write the same way? Russians - from left to right, Jews - from right to left, and there are the Chinese - from top to bottom. You're nothing but bare ignoramuses! Well, oh well, life and time, God willing, will teach you."

Then Nikitich called everyone and said, "This is what needs to be done, this is how I figure it out." - and whispered to his friends standing around holding each other by the shoulders. In the morning, the entire team in ceremonial armor and the girls in elegant dresses stood in front of the gates of Kashchei's Castle.

Dobrynya shouted as loudly as he could, "Come out, Kashchei, we need to have a conversation! And if you don't come out, then come to the field behind the Castle at noon — we will fight you to the death!" A silence fell such as the world had never known: the wind died down, the trees didn't rustle, the birds didn't sing, the river did not babble, and the water in the moat around the castle seemed to have fallen into a deathly stillness. I don't know how long the boys and girls stood at the gates, but suddenly, the bridge across the moat was lowered with a roar, the gates swung open, and Koshchei the Deathless himself rode out on a huge black horse. He was dressed head to toe in armor, with a helmet visor lowered and gloves on his hands - neither his hands nor his face were visible.

He dismounted slowly with dignity, then stood opposite Dobrynya, straightening his shoulders in a black cloak – like a monuments, nothing more, nothing less. He drew his sword from its sheath, swung it and . drove it into the ground up to the hilt.

He raised the visor and walked slowly in front of the whole crowd, like a seasoned military leader, looking each person intently in the eyes. He thought for a moment, then took Vasilisa out of the line, looked her over from head to toe and said: "You are a beautiful maiden, no doubt about it. I have never seen such beauty in my entire long life!

I know that my sister Yaga sent me to fight. All her life she was not known for her intelligence in our family, and now she has apparently gone completely mad. You cannot kill me - after all, I am immortal. That whole tale about the chest, the hare, the duck, and the egg? I made it up myself, just to keep young men like you who roam the forests from bothering me … and so that they themselves would not die in battle against me.

I do not like to kill - I am kind." Having finished his speech, he approached the heroes, bowed to them at the waist, and then, turning to Alyosha Popovich, said: "It is the pure truth of what Dobrynya told you. I am an enchanted Prince, and I wear armor so as not to frighten the people, my face is too terrible to behold. But, I love you, Alyosha! I have no need for beautiful maidens. You alone are my destiny.

My betrothed! And if you love me, then give me your hand, and I will take you to my home." Everyone fell silent, taken aback by such a speech. Alyosha looked long and deeply into Kashchei's beautiful blue eyes, glanced at Vasilisa questioningly, to which she nodded her sweet head in response.

Then Alyosha extended his hand to Kashchei, and he took it in his palms. At that very moment, a great miracle occurred - the armor, helmet, and gloves disappeared, and a prince of unprecedented beauty appeared before everyone, put his arm around Alyosha's shoulders and led him into his tower, which stood in place of the Castle.

And as soon as the doors of the tower closed, somewhere deep in the forest, something crashed, as if an old tree had fallen to the ground, and a voice cried out: "Oy, gevalt!" No one understood a thing; it was just empty noise, and that was all. Then Dobrynya Nikitich quietly croaked into his mustache, but no one paid attention to it.

. . . .

Many years have passed since then. Dobrynya and Marya settled in Kyiv, and Ilya and Varvara in Murom. And they had children, grandsons and granddaughters in great numbers. They lived happily ever after and never told anyone how they went to war with Kashchei the Deathless.

No one heard anything about Kashchei and Alyosha, only I remember one person once saying that they sailed across the Great Ocean and settled there in what is called the West of North America. Our Vasilisa was less fortunate – she married Ivanushka the Fool and wanted to make a smart man out of him. They say she dipped him in a vat of boiling water, and then in a vat of ice water, but it was no use. So she suffered all her life with Ivan, although she loved Kashchei until the end of her days.

Oh, I almost forgot. Do you remember that rumble in the forest? That was Baba Yaga. She fell in her mortar from the sky straight to the ground, and into the beautiful woman she had been before, and cried out in her native language: "Oh, gevalt"! People say that from then on she began to be called Margarita and that she went into service to the Master, with whom she remains to this day.

Parable

For many years, Bolt and Nut had lived in perfect harmony. Pressed tightly together, they loved to whisper quietly, calling themselves by various funny names. Only two large beams, which they held on top of a pole, knew this secret of theirs. These beams were decent individuals and did not tell anyone about Bolt and Nut's secret. The secret was also known to the old, creaky Washer, who was Bolt's mother-in-law. Every now and then, she complained about her lonely life and lectured our heroes, to which they, loving each other, did not pay much attention.

One night, a hurricane-force wind arose. Bolt and Nut clung together tighter than ever, holding fast to the beams on which the electric wires hung. The wind rocked the entire structure but could do nothing to break their grip. Nut and Bolt were stronger than the storm. However, the old squabble, Puck, always dissatisfied with everything, managed to nudge itself just enough to slightly loosen and damage one of Bolt's threads. The hurricane calmed down and everything seemed to return to normal. Butone autumn, Aunt Rust came to visit Bolt and Nut. She stayed for a week, chatted with Puck, and flew away on her rusty business. Several months passed, and in the depths of winter, during a snowstorm, Bolt felt that his strength was running out. With a strong gust of wind, his head came off, and unable to bear the enormous load, the entire structure collapsed to the ground.

The grumpy Puck flew far from the pole and fell into a large icy puddle, where she rusted through and, over time, crumbled to dust. While repairing the pole, the old craftsman found Bolt and Nut, and nearby he also found a head, which he welded to the leg and put in a box with various junk – perhaps it would come in handy. And so, Bolt and Nut ended up together again, lying in a hardware box for many, many years.

Love and devotion always win.

Tikhon

This story began in the summer of 1976. On July 31, on Chkalov Street in Moscow, not far from Kursky Station, near the Glavmosoblstroy building, adults were crowding around, waiting for their children to return from the second shift at the Gaidar Pioneer Camp. A column of buses and two trucks with suitcases slowly crawled up to the tall grey building and, sighing with their brakes, froze in place. It was four o'clock in the afternoon, and the July heat was in full force. Gusts of wind chased scraps of newspapers across the street like boys kicking torn balls in the courtyards of Moscow

The doors of the buses swung open, and the children poured out onto the sidewalk. Their confinement in nature was over. The fathers vigilantly scanned the area, eager to be the first to notice any danger and stop it. The mothers fussed over their children, inspecting them for scratches and bruises, as if they could be avoided after nearly a month of free-range childhood adventures. My wife and I were waiting for our six-year-old son, Vitka, to return from his four-week stay at a pioneer camp. Sveta, my wife, stood at the door of the bus with the sign "10th Squad" and was noticeably nervous. I headed over to the trucks with the luggage and, five minutes later, rejoined the group waiting by the bus. The tenth squad consisted of thirty-two boys and girls, all six and seven years old. The children, with the help of a counselor, slowly descended the steps of the bus onto the sidewalk, immediately falling into the arms of their parents.

This process dragged on for what felt like an eternity. The tanned children crawled out of the doorway and, having fallen into the arms of their parents, dissolved into the anthill of adults crowded along the facade of Glavmosoblstroy. My wife and I counted thirty-one children who had left the bus, but Vitya was still nowhere to be seen.

Finally, our son's back appeared in the doorway, and then his hands. He was carefully dragging a half-torn oilcloth bag down the steps, in which something was moving. I hurried to help, grabbing my son with one hand and the bag with the other, and carefully placed the precious burden on the sidewalk. At that moment, the group leader spoke in a stern, instructive tone:

- "Viktor Naumov, I forbade you to bring this animal into the city! And what are you going to do now?" the group leader demanded sternly.

The boy looked at me and my wife guiltily and remained silent, his head bowed. In front of us stood a son who had clearly grown up, but he no longer looked like the city boy we had sent to camp at the beginning of July. Instead, he looked like a small village man. He had grown a centimeter or two, which made me very happy: he was just like me and my one hundred and ninety-one centimeters tall. Keep it up, I thought. Neither Sveta nor I were prepared for such a transformation, and Vitka immediately sensed this. He leaned over and unzipped the bag.

- "Parents, I brought us a puppy."

He emphasized the word to us. A homegrown diplomat! At that moment, I realized that my son knew us better than we knew him. Shifting my gaze from Vitka to the bag, from which the puppy's black, shaggy muzzle appeared, I lifted the oilcloth rag. The head licked my hand, as if to say:

- Hi, man.

The puppy looked about three months old and weighed six or seven kilograms. Vitka stroked the shaggy creature and proudly said:

- "He's two and a half months old. His name is Tikhon. He's a mix of a wolfhound and a wolf!"

All Sveta could squeeze out after this announcement was, - "This is all we needed."

Oh, God, our grave sins. We caught a taxi and went home.

The car pulled up to our entrance at half past five. As we got out of the taxi, we watched Vitya with interest. He got out of the car, pulled out a bag and opened the zipper all the way.

A shaggy creature of black color with grayish-tan markings on both sides and brown ears crawled out. After floundering, it sat down onto the grass of the lawn and stared at Vitya. The boy pulled a worn rope out of the bag and, looping it gently around the dog's neck, said:

- Let's go for a walk.

The dog obediently trudged after Vityok. Approaching a stunted tree that grew in the middle of the lawn, the son commanded:

- Do your business!

Tikhon sniffed the tree and quickly relieved himself.

Vitya ordered again:

- Let's go home! - And he pulled the puppy towards the lawn fence.

They both deftly jumped over the low fence and headed towards our entrance. We followed them. Having climbed the stairs to the second floor, the whole family entered the apartment. Vityok removed the noose from the puppy's neck and he, without hesitation, ran straight into his son's room. Stopping in the middle, he raised his head, sniffed the air, and immediately headed to the corner where a desk stood by the window. Having spun around a couple of times in place, Tikhon plopped down on the floor, resting his head on his front paws and closing his eyes. We understood - this meant that the dog had found his place. Vitek rummaged in his pants pocket and pulled out something wrapped in a newspaper.

- Mom, - he said, - Tikhon should eat on schedule, twice a day: at seven in the morning and at seven in the evening. This is his dinner. - Then he unfolded the newspaper, revealing a piece of boiled meat and a marrow bone. - Where did you get this "wealth"? - Sveta asked.

- The cook, Aunt Nastya, gave it to me for the road. - Vitya answered. - Mom, I will need a bowl for water and a bowl for food. I will explain to you later what Tikhon should eat.

The son put the suitcase on his bed, opened it, and began to carefully take out things and put them on the shelves in his closet. Sveta and I were too amazed to come to our senses -: our child had been swapped.

A boy who knew how to throw things around like no one else had gone to camp, and he returned as a neat freak. Not only were all the things folded, they were washed and ironed. A miracle, and nothing less! And Vityok, continuing to put away his clothes, was looking for something in the suitcase. Sveta was speechless, and I couldn't help but ask:

- Who washed and ironed your clothes?

- I did it myself. – My son answered. – I helped Aunt Nastya in the kitchen, and in return she fed me and helped me look after Tishka. Well, and at the same time taught me how to wash and iron. She is elderly, lonely woman – I felt sorry for her, so I helped her in the kitchen and trained Tikhon in my free time.

- What are you looking for in the suitcase? – Sveta asked.

- An old belt. I want to make a collar for Tishka out of it because the rope is rubbing his neck.

We just looked at each other, understanding each other without words: our son had matured by at least a year that month.

- Dad, – Vitek said, – I need an alarm clock to walk Tishka by the hour.

The next day, Sunday, the alarm clock woke us up at six in the morning. Vitek took the dog for a walk.

On Monday, after work, I stopped at a pet store and bought bowls for water and food, and a beautiful leather collar with a leash. When I gave all these things to my son, his eyes shone with such joy that I had not seen since Sveta and I gave him a bicycle for his birthday.

Three weeks passed. Our son took full responsibility for the dog's care. The only thing that was required of us, that is, of my wife, was food for the dog. Vitek fed and walked the dog by the hour and spent two hours training him, teaching the puppy various commands. Our son's room, which previously resembled a warehouse of sticks, nails, scrap metal, and other junk, transformed into a model room fit for a junior soldier. No, don't think that the screws and nuts have disappeared — they simply found a place for themselves, freeing up space for the puppy.

And Tishka, like a fairy-tale hero, grew by leaps and bounds. The size of his paws was already larger than Svetlana's hands, and I thought with horror about how big this shaggy creature — with a black muzzle but very kind eyes — would become when fully grown. Speaking of Tishka's eyes: one evening, while playing with him, I noticed a small wound in the corner of his left eye. Several days passed, but the red spot clearly became larger and more visible. On Friday evening, before going to bed, I went into my son's room and asked:

- Vitek, have you noticed that the wound near Tishka's eye is getting bigger and bigger?

- "Yes, dad," - He answered. - "I wash his eye with warm water three times a day, but the wound does not get smaller. And sometimes he whines when he rubs his eye with his paw."
- "Look here, Victor, I'll ask aunt Irina to go to the vet with Tikhon on Monday. She's a teacher and still on vacation. I'm sure she won't refuse. The doctor will also give him all the necessary vaccinations. You'll go with her. Do you agree?"

- "Yes, Dad." - Myson answered.

On Monday evening, returning from work, I saw my son sitting on a bench near our entrance. He was obviously waiting for me, and when I approached, he said:

- Dad, I need to tell you something.

- I'll listen to you, but before that, I need to tell you that Irina called me after a visit to the vet. The doctor gave Tikhon all the necessary vaccinations, but they decided to keep him at the clinic for at least a week to treat the wound near his eye.

- "Yes, Dad, I know that aunt Irina called you." - My son spoke in a mature manner. - "I need to tell you how I met Tishka."

- Wouldn't you like to tell this to Mom and me? - I asked.

- No. - He snapped. - This is a strictly man-to-man conversation. I'll tell you, and you decide for yourself whether to tell Mom or not. - Vityok said, looking me straight in the eye.

- Okay, son. - I answered. - I'm listening to you.

Vitya thought for a moment and then spoke:

- It all started a week after we arrived at the camp. I was assigned to the kitchen duty team. The next day, at six in the morning, seven people from different squads lined up outside the kitchen. The head cook, Aunt Nastya, explained what we needed to do and told me that, as the youngest, I would be on standby to assist her.

By nine o'clock, the camp had been served breakfast, and cook Nastya called all the helpers to the table to have a snack. Once everyone had gathered at the table, she called me aside and said:

- You and I must first feed all the workers, and only then will we eat.

It was lively at the table. The cook's helpers and the kids were wolfing down their breakfast. And when everyone had eaten their fill and gone their separate ways, Nastya said to me:

- Now it's time for you and me to eat. Here, take two bowls and bring them to the dogs while I cook some eggs. See over there, on the hillock? That old house is the hut of our night watchman, Spiridon.

Over there, by the camp fence, is the kennel of our dog, Mashka. She gave birth to puppies a month and a half ago. All the puppies have been taken and only one is left, the biggest and shaggiest, named Tikhon. Give them something to eat and pour some fresh water into the bowls lying by the kennel.

I was about twenty meters from the kennel when I saw Spiridon. He was drunk. In one hand he had an open bottle of vodka and in the other a stick, with which he was trying to hit Mashka. I stopped dead in my tracks and put the bowls of food on the grass, not knowing what to do. And Spiridon continued to scold the dogs.

Tishka clearly did not like this, and he trotted to help his mother, deftly grabbing the guard's trouser leg with his teeth and pulling it back with all his might. But Spiridon, having managed to free himself, hit the puppy in the eye with the toe of his boot. Tikhon yelped in pain and crawled to the kennel. And then I did a very bad thing: picking up a stick with a rusty nail that was lying by the fence, ran towards the guard, and shouted that I would kill him if he did not leave the dogs alone. Spiridon simply dropped the piece of wood, turned around and, staggering, walked through the gate to his house, loudly cursing and shouting something like:

- The city scum has come here in droves!

Only Nastya, who was standing in the kitchen doorway, saw everything that had happened. - Okay, - I said, - we won't tell Mom anything. You're right - this is really a man's conversation.

We went to the door of our apartment, and I said:

Son, you did absolutely the right thing, like a real man.

That evening, having told Sveta about the conversation with Vitya, I suggested to my wife that we keep this story a secret.

The next day, when Sveta was busy in the kitchen preparing dinner, Vityok came up to me and said in a very serious tone:

- Dad, when I grow up, I will be a doctor. You can tell Mom everything. - He turned around and, without waiting for my reaction, went to his room. He refused dinner that evening.

Three days later, the veterinarian called me and asked me to come see him. We agreed on the following Saturday. That day turned out to be windy and rainy. On the way to the veterinarian, whom I always called the "dog doctor" , I was overcome by uneasy thoughts.

And my premonitions proved correct. Tikhon greeted me joyfully, wagging his fluffy tail. His left eye was covered with a gauze pad, and he himself resembled a pirate, except without a Sabre. The doctor patted him behind the ear and invited me to sit down. After pacing to the window and back, he took a seat across from me and began to speak:

I have bad news for you. The puppy was mercilessly beaten during the first six weeks of its life, often kicked. During one of those beatings, a tick got into the wound near his eye. Ticks are a terrible danger to animals. They burrow into the wounds and infect the blood. I removed the insect, but the damage had already been done. The puppy will suffer for another five or six weeks, and then…he'll die. I am very sorry, but I have done everything that can be done, and there's nothing more I can do. I strongly recommend putting him to sleep – sooner rather than later. The doctor fell silent, stood up, and left the office, leaving me alone with Tikhon. And Tikhon, as if he understood what had just been said, looked into my eyes and, as if to say:

- Well, man, make a decision. I'm not here to advise you. My death won't be on your conscience: you'd simply be sparing me from suffering. But you have two very serious matters ahead of you: a conversation with your son and, God willing, an explanation with my attacker, the guard Spiridon.

They say that dogs can't hold a person's gaze. That's not true! Tishka and I looked into each other's eyes, and I was the first to look away. About half an hour later, Dr. Shapiro returned to the office. I looked at Tikhon, then met the vet's eyes and finally managed to say:

- Put him to sleep.

I walked home from the dog hospital, trying to figure out what to say to Vitka. Two hours later, soaking wet, I finally trudged through the door , still unable to figure out how to talk to my son. Vitya and his friend were tinkering with something in his room. After telling Sveta what happened at the vet's, I looked at her for a long time, and she only asked:

- What should we do with Vitka?

To which I only shrugged my shoulders. In the evening, I told my son that Dr. Shapiro had called me and said that Tikhon should be under observation for at least three more weeks, and that we could visit him in about ten days. I was buying time, simply not knowing what else to do. At nine in the evening, my son went to bed.

My wife and I watched TV until eleven, still undecided about what to do, before finally falling into bed. It was just after one in the morning, but sleep would not come. I went out to the kitchen, poured a glass of water from the tap, and sat down at the table. A couple of minutes later Vitek appeared in the doorway. He came up to me and, with eyes full of tears, said:

- Dad, I understand everything. - He turned and went to his room.

The next day, Tikhon's bowls, collar, and leash disappeared without a trace. We never returned to the conversation about the fate of the shaggy puppy.

A year passed. Our son finished first grade and went back to the second shift at the Gaidar Pioneer Camp. That year, disaster struck the Moscow region: peat bogs were burning.

Even in Moscow itself, it was sometimes difficult to breathe. The air was saturated with soot, but it was almost impossible to extinguish the fires – peat bogs had to burn all the way through. The fires could have been put out by heavy rain, but there was a drought in the Moscow region. From our friends, we learned that conditions near the camp were even worse than in Moscow, so we decided to bring our son home. The following Saturday, we took the train, and after a couple of hours of traveling and walking, we found ourselves in front of the camp gates.

After finding out that Vitek was on duty in the kitchen, my wife and I divided the responsibilities: Sveta went to draw up paperwork with the camp administration and collect her son's things, and I went to get Vitya. The canteen and kitchen building were in the far corner of the camp grounds, about a five-minute walk from the First Squad's house. The children on duty in the kitchen were running around the canteen hall, setting the tables for dinner. Vityok saw me and, running up, blurted out:

- What happened? What are you doing here?

I barely recognized my son. Vitya had some kind of crazy look. A strong smell of burning hung in the air and was clearly affecting the boys.

- Mom and I came to take you away from here. - I answered.

- That's great! - He yelled. - Dad, we're just suffocating here. Six people have already been taken from our squad, and two more ended up in the hospital.

I don't know why, but at that moment it seemed to dawn on me and I said:

- Vityok, you finish your business, and I would like to look at Mashka. Is that possible?

- Yes, her kennel is over there. - And he pointed his finger at the open window.

I spotted a doghouse tucked in the corner of the fence and walked toward it across the flattened, withered grass. The dog lay near its house, breathing heavily, its tongue hanging out. The peat fire was troubling not only people but all the animals in the area.

An empty water bowl was lying next to the doghouse. At that moment, the gate swung open, and a creature about one and a half meters tall tumbled inside rather than walked in. He was a man of about sixty, the kind we often call "one meter with a cap." In one hand, he held an open bottle of vodka, while the other gripped the fence, trying to keep his balance as he squatted slightly:

- Who are you? Outsiders are not allowed! - He said, stumbling on the letter "r".

I felt like I was about to crush this bastard, but I restrained myself and said:

- Bring the dog some water.

- What did you say?! I'll... - He swayed and sank down right by the fence.

Being two heads taller than this abomination, I could no longer restrain myself. Grabbing him by the chest with one hand, I snatched a bottle of vodka and poured it on his head:

- Listen to me, you cheapskate —bring the dog some water right now! - I didn't speak, I hissed, and it clearly worked.

He took off like a sprinter at the start, and a couple of minutes later, returned with a jug of cold water from the house. I filled Mashka's bowl, and she greedily lapped it up to the bottom.

- Listen to me carefully, Spiridon, - I continued to hiss. - Every single day, you will make sure the dog has water and food. And if you disobey, I will find you, dig you out from underground , and hang you by the collar on this very fence, near the kennel.

I probably looked scary, and the vodka did not add courage to Spiridon:

- Yes sir! - I heard in response and with difficulty restrained myself from cackling.

That evening we got home and a week later our son again looked like himself.

. . . .

Four years passed. Sveta, Vityok and I left the Soviet Union and settled in America. My son became a doctor. Several generations of dogs lived in his house, but not one of them was ever named Tikhon. And Russia still drinks its bitter sorrow, continuing to drink itself to death...

Barrack #6

It was the summer of 1962. Kurt Janis sat on a grassy slope above a mountain river, smoking a pipe and lazily sipping beer from a bottle. The early June heat in this part of German Silesia was unusually intense. There was a sense of laziness in everything: the grass moved lazily, the white clouds crawled slowly across the light blue sky, the treetops creaked lazily with their branches and rustled their leaves.

The birds hid from the heat, waiting for the sunset. After rinsing his face and neck with lukewarm water from a flask that had warmed up from the heat, which brought some relief, Kurt leaned his back against a tree and, moving his Tyrolean cap with a feather onto his nose, dozed off.

He liked to come here to rest. Hearing the thunder of an explosion in a quarry located two kilometers from here, he glanced at his watch, stood up with ease , brushed off his uniform, and began walking toward the labor camp for teenagers aged ten to sixteen. This top-secret facility was called Youth, and the motto above the gates read: "SURVIVE THE STRONGEST". SS Major Janis was the commandant of this camp. The staff consisted of two platoons of guards and SS women; none ranked below corporal.

The camp area, spread out in the mountains above a fast-flowing river and surrounded by a double fence made of electrified barbed wire, was shaped like a pentagon. At each corner stood an observation tower, and the gates were on the southern and northern sides. Within this hellish pentagon stood ten barracks for prisoners, each built to hold fifty people, along with a separate kitchen and a two-story commandant's office, with Janis's office and the chancery on the second floor; the medical unit was on the first. Beneath it, in the basement, strange experiments were carried out. From that basement „ came the smell of chemicals, and at night, the muffled screams of prisoners could be heard. The children chosen for the experiments never returned to the barracks.

Those children were never seen alive again. Behind the fence, not far from the southern gate, five wooden cottages stood in a row – housing for the service personnel, the guards' barracks, and the commandant's house. The daily routine was scheduled down to the minute. Wake up at four thirty, breakfast at five hundred hours, work in the quarry from six thirty to nineteen thirty, dinner at eight hundred hours, lights out at nine thirty. A single day off – on the second Sunday of every month. Roll call was held four times a day. In this camp, no one was gassed or cremated.

There were neither gas chambers nor crematoria in the camp. The prisoners themselves loaded the bodies of those who died – whether from starvation, quarry accidents, or execution – onto carts. This grim task was carried out daily, as the carts were wheeled between the rows of barbed wire to the northern gate, where the bodies were dumped into a passive pit, six hundred by six hundred meters, enclosed by a three-meter deep fence.

The remains were covered with slaked lime, and two days later, a very thick layer of soil was poured over them. Shrubs were then planted on top. From a bird's-eye view, this place looked like an ordinary green area. The only road made of compacted gravel, winding through a mountain crevice, approached the camp gates from the south.

There was no punishment cell or corporal punishment here, although the guards occasionally struck a teenager with a whip once or twice, but the children took it as encouragement. Any violation of discipline or order was punishable by execution – carried out by the firing squad during the evening roll call. Only one officer, Kurt Janis, carried out these executions . The offender would kneel, facing the prisoners, and the commandant would deliver a single shot to the back of the head with his Luger.

This camp was created on the personal directive of Reich Fuehrer SS Himmler, with one single purpose - to calculate the survival rate of boys subjected to hard labor in the quarries.

There was another important rule that the boys did not know about - children who reached the age of sixteen were not released from imprisonment; instead, they were transferred to a regular labor camp. The Yunost concentration camp had already existed for a whole year, but none of the boys lived to be sixteen. The prisoners were international, including even Jews and gypsies.

On June 10, 1943, thirty-three teenagers lived in Barrack No. 6, which stood approximately in the middle of the row of wooden buildings. New arrivals came at the end of each month, and meals were delivered to the barracks on a count of fifty inmates, so that for almost three weeks until the end of June, the teenagers in Barrack No. 6 would receive an extra ration. Food meant strength, which the boys were losing more and more every day. The population of Barrack No. 6 consisted almost entirely of Ukrainians and Poles, along with two Czechs, three Romanians and one Jewish boy.

This boy's name was Emil, and he was thirteen years old. He had lived in this barrack since January of 1942. In the first year, the population of Barack. 6, nicknamed "The Kennel" by the boys from the first day – had completely turned over. Only puny little Milya remained alive. Ryzhik, as the boys called him because of the color of his hair, eyebrows, and the freckles that covered his face, had amazing gray eyes that no one could stand. Milya often looked at the sky for a long time and quietly whispered something, as if he were talking to someone up there, high above the clouds. The boys heard one guard tell another, pointing her finger at Emil, that his entire family – mother, father, and three sisters – had been executed before his eyes. And still, the boys of Barrack No. 6 never ceased to be amazed at how this small, puny boy, even by camp standards, who worked on par with everyone else, was still alive. When they asked him where he got his strength from, he looked up to the sky and answered: "From there." The boys just laughed - they had all long since lost their faith in God. By some twist of fate, the one closest to Milka was a Polish boy named Vacek. This boy was a head taller than all the teenagers and, of course, stronger than all of them, for which the camp commandant appointed him the head of the barracks.

Vacek commanded the boys and punished them for minor violations. He usually did this with a blow to the teeth, but did not hit very hard. He called Emil a "little Jew" and regularly used his fist as a tool to "educate" him. Once, while working in a quarry, Vacek made a fatal mistake - while carrying stones, he stumbled, twisted his leg and sat down for about five minutes to wait until the severe pain passed. Noticing this, the warden ordered him to immediately continue working, reinforcing her order with a blow of the whip. The boy got up and, overcoming the pain, returned to his work. Upon returning to the camp, Fat Elsa, as the boys nicknamed Fat Bitch, reported the incident to the commandant. During the evening roll call, Major Janis, as usual, walked the line of prisoners lined up in front of the barracks.

The boys from the sixth heard the commandant use his Luger twice, at the first barrack, and another shot rang out at barrack number 4. At building number 5, the pistol remained in its holster. The major slowly approached barrack number 6 and stopped in front of the line. Digging the ground with the toe of his boot, he called Vacek out of the line. He looked at him carefully and ordered him to kneel down facing the prisoners.

The boy did as he was ordered and, kneeling down, glanced at Milya, who was standing directly opposite the commandant, as if saying goodbye to him. Ryzhik raised his eyes to the starry evening sky, then turned his gaze to Janis and, catching his gaze, began to stare into the SS man's eyes. Silence fell. Even the wind died down, as if hiding behind the thick bushes that grew outside the camp along the barbed wire. The eyes of everyone standing on the parade ground stared at the commandant's hand, in which he clutched a black Luger aimed at the back of the boy's head.

Major Janis himself could not understand what was happening to him. Instead of pulling the trigger and moving to the next barrack, he stood frozen, as if petrified, unable to move.

The piercing gaze of the huge eyes of the boy standing before him seemed to paralyze both his will and his mind. This lasted no more than a minute, but it seemed like an eternity to Janis. He suddenly ordered Vacek to stand in line and commanded the elders to separate the prisoners back into their barracks.

The boys silently dispersed. When dinner was brought, no one in Barrack No. 6 touched their food. Milya was lying on the top bunk and staring at the ceiling without blinking. Vacek went up to the boy lying under Ryzhik' s place and asked him to change places with him. He laid out his bed under Milka's place, lay down on his side, and went quiet. From that day on, no one ever heard Vacek utter the words "little Jew" again.

A year passed. Children continued to die from rock falls in the quarry and from exhaustion, but the SS man's pistol remained silent. Major Janis withdrew into himself, stopped communicating with anyone unless his duty required it, and in the evenings, instead of his favorite works of Wagner, the music of Bach and Handel could be heard from his bedroom windows.

The boys from barracks No. 6 did not ask questions when they saw Ryzhik go to the window after lights out and look for a long time, either at the stars or at the camp commandant's house. It was clear to everyone that some invisible thread connected the boy with the sky, but no one dared to ask him questions. One chilly November day in 1944, Emil suddenly told Vacek that he would be leaving the camp the following Saturday, and invited the boy to go with him. Vacek asked Ryzhik how he was going to escape from the zone and where they would go, to which Milya replied:

- Just tell me: are you coming with me or not, and don't worry about the rest.

Without knowing why, Vacek nodded his head in response.

On Saturday, at ten o'clock in the evening, when the camp had quieted down, Emil quietly said to Vacek:

- Let's go.

Putting on prisoner jackets and striped caps that resembled skullcaps, they slipped out of the barracks and headed for the southern gate. The parade ground was empty - only four guards and a squad of sentries on towers with searchlights, the beams of which wandered across the entire territory of the camp. Milya approached the guard and ordered him to open the gate.

The guard obeyed and swung open the ominous doors. The escapees went outside the fence, and the guards, having closed the gate, continued to observe the territory of the camp. Vacek could not recover from his amazement. Ryzhik looked back at the gate, and the fugitives confidently headed toward the commandant's house.

The front door wasn't locked. They pushed it open and stepped into the hallway. Music was heard from the second floor - it was Bach's Brandenburg Concerto. - "Wait for me here," Emil said, then climbed the stairs and disappeared into the semi-darkness. Fear and curiosity made Vacek follow Ryzhik, but suddenly he stopped, hiding behind the slightly ajar door, watching silently as events unfolded in the bedroom.

Milya stood in the middle of the room, locking eyes with the commandant. The latter, seated in an armchair with a glass of wine in his hand, as if spellbound, periodically nodded his head in agreement, unable to tear his gaze away from the boy's huge eyes. The encounter lasted no more than five minutes. Then the boy approached the major, took the pistol from the nightstand, and whispered something into his ear. Janis heard only a fragment of a phrase:

- . the time will come, and you will pay for everything.

Having left the commandant's house, the boys walked along the road to the south.

. Kurt Janis awoke suddenly, sensing someone's intense gaze upon him. He stood up, turned around, and saw a man of average height with a balding head and graying temples. He looked about thirty, thirty-five years old. Kurt peered into the stranger's face, feeling that he had seen him somewhere. But where? And the man slowly approached Kurt, chewed his lips and asked:

- Do you remember what I told you on that November night of forty-four? If not, I will remind you. And I told you that the war would soon be over and if you stayed alive, which I'm almost certain of, you would pay for everything! - Emil looked around, thought about something and continued:

- Here's what else I want to tell you. Back at the camp, I was the Angel of Life – saving everyone I could. Now, I've become the Angel of Death. I spent seven long years trying to find you. I traveled all over Europe and, having learned that you had changed your name and were working as a school chemistry teacher, I finally found you here, of all places. The last place I ever expected. Chewing his lips again, Ryzhik took a black Luger out of his pocket:

- Do you remember this thing? Rest assured, I've taken care of your pistol – it works just as flawlessly as it did twenty years ago. I even tested it on Fat Elsa. - Cold sweat ran down the commandant's back. - "Well, then,"- said Emil, in a surprisingly calm tone - "Let's go to the river."

Just like that evening in the fall of '44, Kurt seemed paralyzed, some unknown forces fettered his body. A former career officer, he summoned every ounce of willpower for hand-to-hand combat. But then he met the man's eyes and was overwhelmed by a chilling coldness. There was ice in them. "You will pay for everything!" - pounded in his mind. Following the order, he limply wandered to the cliff.

The stormy stream carried its water about ten meters below them. Emil ordered the SS man, petrified as he had been on the parade ground, to kneel down facing the water. Janis obeyed. Copious tears flowed down his pale, shaved cheeks, though he did not expect a miracle. Amid the roar of the water, no one heard the shot. Kurt's body fell into the water and quickly disappeared between the boulders. The black Luger followed Janis into the water.

Emil walked towards a small grove located two kilometers from the river. He stopped at the edge of the forest near a memorial plaque with the inscription "HERE FROM JANUARY 1942 TO DECEMBER 1944 WAS THE CHILDREN'S CONCENTRATION DEATH CAMP "YUNOST".

There were fresh flowers on the pedestal. Sitting down on a bench nearby, he looked for a long time at the place where there had once been a mass grave, and now a sea of red poppies raged. Then he rose heavily from the bench, raised his hands with clenched fists to the Sky and, directing the gaze of his huge gray eyes to the clouds, whispered something. No one heard him.

From Small to Old

About fifty meters from the trench, lights flashed, followed by the sharp sound of a Kalashnikov's short burst. Barely registering the noise, I felt three strong blows to my chest and was thrown to the opposite wall of the trench. Losing consciousness, I slipped into darkness.

Major Grinko's battalion, suffering heavy losses, covered the division's retreat to the west. Five hundred meters of abyss between a swamp and a river, beyond which there was an impassable quagmire. The trench they dug was only about one and a half meters deep–any deeper was impossible due to groundwater – with a parapet barely twenty centimeters along the edge of the trench. God only knew what kind of protection that offered, especially from snipers entrenched in a copse three hundred meters from our positions.

These shooters, mostly hunters from Siberia, are driving us crazy. They can shoot a squirrel or an arctic fox in the eye from three hundred meters without a telescopic sight. Against us, we're like sitting ducks. Their main targets are our officers and junior commanders. The Russians have plenty of equipment and ammunition, but there is one big problem - the autumn Ukrainian clay. Neither all-terrain vehicles nor tanks can get through this mess: Mother Nature herself is on our side. The only way to the west is an old dirt road that runs roughly along the middle of the isthmus. We must hold this road for seventy-two hours to give our division the opportunity to redeploy to new positions located eighteen kilometers west of our trenches. The Ukrainian army is retreating.

There aren't enough tanks, guns, vehicles, or ammunition. The war has been going on for almost a year. We have suffered heavy losses. The Russians are losing many more people than we are, but they are making up for the shortfall in manpower and equipment very quickly. They have huge reserves, plus Russia is acting according to Stalin's doctrine: one dead soldier is a tragedy, thousands are a strategy. . I am alive, but in shock. All three bullets that hit me in the chest, hit the thick leather belt of my field medic's bag. This belt strap saved my life. I see and hear everything, but it feels distant – like I am watching it all from somewhere outside myself. Darkness has fallen. The battle has died down.

The Russians, lacking tanks and armored personnel carriers, avoid night combat. The first day of defense is coming to an end. I seemed to fly up: the strong hands of the soldiers lifted me out of the water, from the bottom of the trench, put me on a stretcher, and carried me towards the medical battalion, located in the bushes by the river.

The sergeant major of the first company, Vasily Kutsenko, says something to me, but I can't hear him. Let me introduce myself. I am Major Lev Borisovich Borodyansky, head of the division's medical battalion, Medical Service. I am thirty-six years old; I am married and have three children. I live in Kyiv not far from Vladimir skaya Gorka, on Andreev skaya Street, and I am fighting far from home. Actually, I do not fight. I am a surgeon. But when I'm not in surgery or fulfilling my medical duties, I run to the trenches to help the medics.

Today I ran away and ended up under from machine-gun fire I was supposed to leave the front line with the division, but I explained to the chief of staff that I was needed more here. He listened - and allowed me to stay. On my part, this was not heroism - it was simple logic. The covering battalion will have heavy losses and will need a surgeon, and company medics - paramedics. Plus, the medical battalion is stationed nearby , and some of the remaining equipment can be used for operations.

The soldiers carried me to the tent, changed me into dry clothes, and laid me on a field cot — my home for the last two months. I shuddered, woke up, and looked at the clock — it was three in the morning. My hearing had returned; my chest ached. I lifted my undershirt and saw three purple bruises. I carefully sat up on the bed and lowered my legs to the floor, feeling a sharp pain in my torso. Yes, if it weren't for the belt,

I would have been done for. Getting up from the bed, I swayed to the first aid kit, took out two tablets of a strong painkiller and swallowed them with water.

Thanks to the "foreigners" for their help – we received all the medical equipment and medicines from Israel. About twenty minutes later, the pain subsided and I got dressed and went to the battalion commander's tent. Major Grinko, a tall, broad-shouldered man, was sitting at the table, smoking, his head bowed over a map, deep in thought. "What are you thinking about?" - I asked.

- "Where can I get people to hold out for another two days?" - He answered. - "How are you, have you come to? Well, you're lucky: three bullets and all in your belt. By the way, where did you get it? The first aid kit has a thin strap." - He said, looking at me with curiosity.

- "Yes, it broke, and I replaced it with a belt from my shoulder strap." - I answered.

- Sit down, Major, have a sip of vodka. Maybe you can tell me something.

- Yeah, what kind of strategist am I, for God's sake. Thanks for the vodka, but I don't drink.

- How are things with the wounded? - The battalion commander asked.

- Twenty-two people have been sent on carts to the division's new positions. Thirty-six kilometers there and back. They should be back by noon. - I reported.

Why on carts? - Grinko barked. - After all, I ordered the wounded to be sent on two trucks.

- Sorry, Nikolai, I gave you the order. Before I got hit, I told the paramedics to load the wounded soldiers onto the carts. First, we need the vehicles here more urgently. And second, the carts are more reliable - Russian drones don't target them. Forgive me, commander.

Okay. Got it. Next time, let me know, I am the commander here after all. Oh, these paramilitaries! - He said with a slight smile under his mustache. Then he turned back to the table and resumed studying the map. I left the battalion commander's tent and headed to the medical unit. It was five in the morning, dawn would soon break and the meat grinder would begin again. A quiet conversation was heard from the paramedics' tent and I knocked on the strut and stepped inside.

Why aren't you sleeping? - I asked. - You need to rest. There won't be time in a couple of hours.

- Yes, I can't sleep, comrade military doctor. - One of the guys answered. - Nerves.

- I understand, - I said, - rest for another hour, and at six o'clock, zero, I'll be waiting for you in my tent. At six forty-five, full combat readiness. No one is to move to the trenches without my permission. - I ordered and left the tent.

Returning to my bunk, I sat down and wondered where the local population from the farmsteads and the village of Khomki—located two kilometers to the west— had gone. Finding no answer, I got up and went to the operating room. If it weren't for the canvas walls of the tent, you could think that you were in a proper operating room. The equipment and its layout were meticulously planned, with a quality I had never seen before. . Thank you, Israel! I sat down at the table, located in the nook just beyond the operating room and began filling out the information log for the last day, when a guard tore me away from this task.

- Comrade Major, may I speak to you? You have a visitor. - He blurted out.

- Let him come in. - I answered.

A young guy of about seventeen entered the tent, stamped his feet nervously, and said, - Comrade military doctor, may I speak with you?

- Sit down. - I said and pointed to a chair. - Yes, speak.

- We wanted to see the commander, but the guards chased us away. So I made my way to your medical battalion and persuaded the guard to let me see you. - He blurted out.

- Who is this - we? - I asked.

- Local guys. - He answered.

- And are there many of you?

- Yes, five guys.

- What did you want to talk to me about?

- We want to help defend the "ear".

- What, what? - I was surprised.

- "Ear". That's what the locals call the place where you dug the trenches. It's as narrow as the eye of a needle. - He answered.

- And how can you help? What's your name, anyway? - I asked.

- Oles. We're all seventeen years old. They won't take us into the army. We all have double-barreled shotguns and small-bore rifles. Our fathers and older brothers are fighting, and we're sitting at home. If you don't take us into your unit, we'll become partisans ourselves. We won't let the rashists take Ukraine!- He got excited.

- Okay, commander, let's go to the battalion commander.

We left the tent and headed for headquarters. It was still dark. Major Grinko was moving a pencil over the map, assigning tasks to the company commanders. Seeing me and Oles, he addressed the officers , "You're dismissed." - Carry out the order and, looking at us , he said, "I'm already partially informed. Come here. Sit down." And he wearily sank down onto a stool.

- Well, - he turned to me, - what are we going to do with the kids? Send them home? The Russians will be there in two days. - And he turned to Oles, "Where are the mothers and sisters?"

- They went west. - The guy muttered.

- Okay. - The major said, then shouted, "Kutsenko, come to me!" A couple of minutes later, a sergeant major appeared at the entrance to the tent.

- Listen, Vasya, put the guys on rations and send them to the medical battalion to help with the wounded.

- Comrade Major, I have a small drone and a radio. - Oles said. - I know the locations of the trenches and the Russian equipment.

Grinko looked the guy in the eye. - "Okay, you'll stay with me, and the rest of the "team" is at Major Borodyansky's disposal," - the battalion commander ordered.

- Yes. - The sergeant major saluted and left the tent.

The gray morning, washed out by a light rain, began with the Russians' artillery barrage. They fired at random. The scatter of shells howled enormously. They fired from guns dated back to the eighties - clearly firing without precise aim. Of course, we had casualties - killed and wounded- but the Russians could not cause much harm.

The Russians did not dare to attack: the rain had washed out the "ear" even more, and the soldiers slowly walking through the mud would have been an excellent target for our fighters. The day passed relatively calmly, with one problem - snipers, they were "picking off" our command staff here and there. About five snipers were operating on the narrow isthmus.

They were working almost in the open, firing from a distance of about five hundred meters, knowing that we had nothing to respond with. It got dark. The rain subsided. I went to the battalion commander to report on the losses. Entering the commander's tent, I overheard an interesting briefing. Grinko was explaining the mission to Sergeant Major Kutsenko, three fighters from the reconnaissance platoon and. Olesya. Seeing me, he waved his hand, as if to say, "Come, join us at the table." - Sergeant, get the inflatable boat that the Israelis gave us from the warehouse and take the first aid kit from the major. At two o'clock, go up the river toward the Russian positions. Here's a map with the sniper positions - that's Oles with his "fly", that's what he calls his drone, he did his best. He spent two hours flying his "friend" over the Russian positions and found three key points.

- But they won't be there at night. - Kutsenko objected.

- Snipers rarely leave well-established positions. Assistants supply them with food and water. - The battalion commander answered. - Listen carefully to the mission: if we manage to get close to the Russian lines, Oles and his "fly" will confirm the locations of the sniper nests. If the "shooters" are in place, destroy them, and if they are not there, plant mines on their perches. Kutsenko is in charge. If something happens to the kid, it's better not to come back. Questions? - He looked around the group. - Do it.

- Yes, sir! - The sergeant major saluted and everyone left the tent.

- Kutsenko, go get the boat and prepare it. I'll get the medical bag ready. We will meet at the river in an hour.

The sergeant major and his team headed to the warehouse, while I prepared everything necessary for the raid and then went to see the battalion commander. The guard at the commander's tent was reluctant to let me in. - Doctor, the major has gone to rest. He probably hasn't slept for a day.

- Okay, - I said, - I'll come in the morning.

The night was cloudy. Around two in the morning, everyone was ready for the mission. I jumped into the boat with the soldiers and, in response to the silent question of the sergeant major, who looked at me reproachfully, said - the battalion commander has given permission.

Vasily chuckled to himself, he understood everything, but said nothing.

Half an hour later, we moored at a marshy bank. At this point, the river was about a hundred and fifty meters wide. Oles launched the "fly" and send it toward the Russian positions. He did his best, but he couldn't pinpoint the exact location of the snipers' nests. Darkness pressed in around us. We went up the river another hundred meters.

Oles and I landed on a narrow, ten-meter strip of bushes along the river, and the sergeant major and the scouts rowed away from the shore, directing the boat toward the Russian positions, and a minute later melted into the darkness. About thirty meters from the shore, the scouts quietly went into the water, and Kutsenko drove it to the middle of the river and hid. Forty minutes later, an explosion was heard at the Russian positions, followed by a wave of confusion. Another half hour passed, and a boat carrying the sergeant major and three scouts, one of whom was slightly wounded in the arm, moored to the bushes, emerging from the gray-black haze.

Oles and I ducked into the "rubber band," as the soldiers called the inflatable boat , and we slowly, so as not to make noise, headed along the marshy bank toward our positions. Halfway home, the moon emerged from behind the clouds, casting a yellow path along the river and making us as visible as if we were held in the palm of someone's hand. The Russians opened up a barrage of mortar fire and one charge landed in the water, about seven meters from us. The shrapnel spared no one: everyone was slightly "scratched", but Olesya was unlucky – he was badly wounded in the leg. The boat, cut up by shrapnel, slowly but surely sank into the water. We swam the last fifty meters to the shore. What happened at the Russian positions, I only learned once we reached the shore. God exists! On the morning of the third day, the order came to retreat. Our men fortified themselves in new positions and the howitzers opened fire on the "ear", which gave Grinko's battalion the opportunity to abandon their positions and retreat toward the division's new location. Oles was already on the mend in the new medical battalion. I managed to save his leg, but the injury will cause him to limp slightly for the rest of his life.

The next morning, the battalion commander visited me and told me exactly what happened that night. He said the team had caught two snipers on the spot, and the third had gone off to relieve himself. The scout managed to plant a mine on the sniper's perch but didn't have time to retreat. The sniper, upon returning, was blown up by the "surprise", and the soldier's hand was hit by shrapnel. The battalion commander entered the tent with the wounded and, approaching Oles's bed, presented him with an award . Then he stroked the guy's head and said, "Thank you, Sonny. Thank you on behalf of the entire battalion." - And bowing low, he left the medical battalion. Tears glistened in his eyes. That same evening, Major Grinko came into my nook.

- You deserve a slap on the wrist for your recklessness, leaving the battalion without a surgeon! But well, you saved the boy, and for that, thank you. - He patted me on the shoulder and left the tent.

Two weeks later, we recaptured the isthmus and moved further east, toward Donbass. We went slowly, but surely. Major Grinko has since been promoted to lieutenant colonel and now serves as the division's acting chief of staff. Oles and the others work with me in the medical battalion. No one knows when this war, imposed on us by the Kremlin, will end, but it will definitely end in our victory. Because when everyone, from young to old, is fighting, it simply cannot be any other way. I know that for certain.

One Day in Life of
Eduard Yevgenievich

I have two friends: Yashka from apartment three and Vitek from apartment eighteen. They're both six years old, and I am four. Oh right, I apologize – I completely forgot to introduce myself. My name is Eduard Yevgenyevich, named after the Russian hound on my great-grandfather's side. But for some reason, the whole neighborhood calls me Polkan. God bless them.

I am a big shaggy mongrel, brown with yellow markings and a fluffy tail. One ear stands up, the other droops halfway. One eye is dark; the other is light. In short, it is difficult to call me handsome. My family includes German shepherds, Russian hounds, St. Bernards, huskies, a couple of Dobermans and one, excuse me, lapdog. How she got mixed into this crew, I have no idea. Sometimes, sensing her blood, I start whining like a fly caught in a web, struggling in vain to get out. That's, so to speak, my whole story - my dog's Fifth Point is not very important.

I live under the stairs leading to the basement apartment where the janitor lives. Well, she's not exactly a janitor, but the janitor's girl. Her name is Tikhonovna. She is a tall, fat woman with a moustache, who looks more like a man than a woman. Her hands are like two Soviet shovels, she wears size forty-five boots, and her face is often scowling, but she has a very soft heart.

She constantly scolds me for my dirty paws, for my tail, which prevents her from opening the door to her apartment, for my low hoarse bark and, nevertheless, she always keeps a bowl of fresh water in my corner under the stairs and feeds me tasty leftovers from her table. When the cold weather comes, Tikhonovna brings an old torn blanket that smells like home, and on especially harsh nights, she lets me into the hallway at night so that I can warm up. I want to draw your attention to the fact that although I see the world from the height of your hip, I consider myself a pretty intelligent dog. That's something I get from the Dobermans on my father's side. I have no formal education—everything I know and can do is the genetic legacy of my ancestors: anger and fearlessness from the shepherd, endurance from the husky, love for children from the St. Bernard. My two best friends are the boys from our house. I am always with them when they go out to the yard, returning home from kindergarten.

These boys, when they grow up, will probably become researchers, like, say, Przhevalsky. How do I know this name - Przhevalsky? Most likely from the huskies on my grandmother's side, from my mother's family. I remember vividly the steppes and mountains of Central Asia, where I have never been.

Today we are going to explore the ruins of an old estate not far from the tram depot. Yashka and Vitek run to their homes to get flashlights, while I sit down by the garbage in case someone's thrown away something tasty…Ten minutes later, the boys come out into the yard with their pockets mysteriously bulging. After exchanging glances like conspirators, they slowly walk behind the house, as if on a swing, but disappearing from the sight of their mothers watching them from the windows, they jump up and run to the ruins. Out of breath, they reach the fence surrounding the abandoned building, plop down on the grass, take something wrapped in newspaper out of their pockets, unwrap it and. oh, the smell! Yashka has a piece of black bread, poured with sunflower oil, covered with chopped green onions and salt. Vitka has a slice of white bread, thickly spread with butter and generously sprinkled with granulated sugar.

All this is divided in half and chewed with such an appetite that all my calm, this is from my great-grandmother - a St. Bernard, cannot hold me in place. I slowly crawl up to the boys, wagging my eyebrows, up and down, up and down, dropping my head on my front paws. Saliva drips from the corners of my mouth onto the grass, and I'm more like a small horse than a big dog,. My good friends, of course, see the eyes of an eternally hungry creature and, breaking off a piece, hold out this food of the gods to me. Being the very picture of politeness, I carefully take these gifts with my front teeth and chew, savoring each bite slowly. Then, I lick the boys' hands with gratitude and crawl away at a respectful distance, hoping that there is something else hidden in the kids' pockets.

My sense of smell does not fail me - a large green apple appears from a pocket, my beloved Antonovka! Several pieces of this deliciousness fly into the air, and I deftly catch them. The ritual is over. It was a royal dinner! It's time to get down to business and two friends climb over a slanted section of the fence that I can't jump over. I start running along the old fence, hoping to find at least some kind of hole, but alas, there are no holes in the fence.

Time passes, and I keep staring at this insurmountable obstacle, and painfully think about what to do. Suddenly, I see a vole's head appear from under the fence and dart into the grass. "Dumbass," I mutter inwardly, a descendant of two Dobermans, and I begin to furiously dig the ground under the fence.

Ten minutes later, I'm already halfway under the fence, nose-first into the clearing in front of the house. But the other half, excuse me, my butt, having caught on some part of the fence, gets stuck, and I'm shamefully sticking out from under the fence, unable to move forward or backward. At this time, Vitek, having torn himself away from his business, runs up to me and, having instantly assessed my shameful position, picks up a heavy stone from the ground, knocks away the hated picket trapping me. I'm free! Without waiting for gratitude, the boy runs to the other end of the clearing, where Yashka continues to tinker with something. I, having licked my slightly damaged butt, rush to the guys. My curiosity knows no bounds, this I clearly inherited from the lapdog on my aunt's side: ladies are ladies.

I run up and see a large, deep ditch filled with water. This ditch stretches from one end of the clearing to the other, completely blocking the entrance to the old house. There is no way to get around this obstacle, the only option is to swim across. Only now do I realize what my friends have been up to - the boys are constructing a raft. They're piecing it from two torn tires and boards, lying around in abundance in the clearing.

Having connected all this junk with scraps of wire and taking a piece of tattered plywood in their hands, they push their structure into the water, jump onto the raft and, oh miracle, this structure stays afloat. I am rushing along the edge of the ditch, from excitement, not finding a place for myself, and my little travelers, kneeling, begin to row with plywood oars and slowly move towards the "Castle of Monte Cristo". I am overcome with pride in the heirs of Przhevalsky. This is an amazing feeling - pride in your friends. The future explorers of Antarctica and the Sahara are almost halfway across the water obstacle and I, having calmed down, sit down on the grass. Suddenly, right before my eyes, the raft begins to fall apart. Yashka, having fallen into the water, manages to grab onto one of the boards and somehow keeps his head above water, but Vitka's head disappears into the depths and only his little childish hands try to grab onto the tire and climb onto it. Some unknown force throws me up and I splash into the water.

Only later did I realize that it was a St. Bernard on my great-grandfather's side. In ten seconds, I swim up to the torn tire, lower, pardon me, my muzzle under the water, grab Vitka by the collar of his shirt and, holding his head above water, swim to the edge of the ditch and pull him out onto the grass. The boy, having swallowed water, is breathing heavily, and I throw myself into the ditch again and swim as fast as I can to Yasha, who is still staying afloat, clutching a piece of board. I grab the end of the piece of wood with my teeth, drag it along with the boy to the shore and, having reached it, we both crawl out onto the green slope. Having made sure that the children are okay, I crawl under the fence and rush, thanks to the Russian hound in my blood, to Tikhonovna.

Thank God she is in the yard. I bark desperately and pull her by the apron behind the house. At first, she hits me with a broom, but, sensing that something is wrong, she rushes after me. Four men who were hammering "Goat" on a table in the middle of the yard rush after us. We run to the old estate. The men quickly break down the fence and rush to the children.

The boys, having caught a little of their breath, sit on the grass with tears in their eyes. The children are picked up and carefully carried home, and Tikhonovna has already called the policeman with her whistle. Everyone left, and I lay down on the grass to catch my breath and dry off a little. The children were saved, and no one cared about me, a mongrel.

Having dried off, in the evening I trotted slowly into the yard under my stairs, thinking about the sad fate of the mongrel named Polkan. I slowly enter the yard full of residents discussing the incident. Seeing the shaggy monster, people who had previously paid no attention to me, and some who had driven me away when I was too close, now try to pet me and tug at my ears. "Here's the thing," I say to myself, "Dear Eduard Yevgenyevich, now you are not just a mongrel, but a Yard Dog, and that, by our canine standards, oh, how much it means. But you people, of course, will not understand this."